Enlightened

Book Three
Duty and Deception

By
JL Redington

© JL Redington 2015

No part of this publication may be reproduced, or stored in a retrieval system, or transmitted in any form or by any means, electronic, mechanical, photocopying, recording or otherwise without written permission of the author.

Table of Content

Prologue
Chapter One
Chapter Two
Chapter Three
Chapter Four
Chapter Five
Chapter Six
Chapter Seven
Chapter Eight
Chapter Nine
Chapter Ten
Chapter Eleven
Chapter Twelve
Chapter Thirteen
Epilogue
Preview

Prologue

Wesley Tipton sat alone in a cheap motel room musing at the odds of his daughter, Sophia, adopted at birth, hooking up with the likes of Justin Markham, now known as Neo Weston. Worlds apart, not even working in the same *city*, yet they did meet and now they were married. Tipton marveled at Neo's ability to keep that relationship so well hidden from both the Bureau and the NSA leadership. That whole situation irritated him beyond belief.

Wesley had no idea he'd even fathered a child, and now she was an adult. That was an incredibly difficult thing for him to wrap his head around. All these years he'd been a father. *How do I reconcile something like that?*

However, what truly perplexed him was how his group of rogue agents changed Justin's appearance, wiped his memory, moved him across the country and yet Neo and Sophia *still* found their way back to each other. The two of them were like the proverbial moth and flame; only this flame wasn't the destructive type.

It was the kind that burned inside you, so hot you feared it would consume you, body and soul.

He'd known that kind of love once. One time in his life he'd known that kind of love, and his broken heart would never be mended. That flame was extinguished years ago, when Sophia's mother was killed, but it still caused an ache in him that often made him want to tear his gut out of his body to stop the pain.

Now he sat in a cheap, dirty motel room, friendless and alone. This is *not* how he thought his life would go. But he had ideas. He had a plan, of sorts. Actually he had about three different plans. Which one he chose depended on how he wanted his life to play out from this point. That was just the way he liked it. He had control of his life and he preferred it that way. Now, which plan to choose? That was going to take some thought.

Chapter One

Elsa. Elsa was so beautiful. She was Swedish and was blessed with the beauty of the Swedish people. With amazingly soft, thick blonde hair, piercing blue eyes that could light up a sky, she possessed the face of a model. She could've *been* a model had she chosen, but not his Elsa. She was too wild, too passionate for modeling. She needed excitement, the thrill of the hunt, the ecstasy of the invisible kill. These things only served to make her more heated and thrilling in bed. She was like a wild tigress, unable to contain herself, unwilling to do so. Wesley gasped at the memory. She was still so much a part of him.

Wesley Tipton sat on the dilapidated bed, savoring the memory of the woman who'd born his child. He hadn't known of the pregnancy. He and Elsa were very in love, even though they only saw each other once every eighteen months or so. Their unorthodox jobs kept them apart. These ops weren't the eight-to-five kind of job with weekends off. Their assignments were dangerous and often life threatening and when they were working, their assignments consumed them, body and soul.

It broke his heart she'd been pregnant on her own, alone, without his support, even having the baby alone. She was worthy of so much more. When he heard she'd been arrested, he feared the worst for her and for good reason. Did he run to her aid? Try to rescue her? No, that was not their way. She would want him to live, to continue on in their chosen 'career.' She would have been furious with him for putting himself in danger for her. He stayed away out of respect for Elsa. At least, that's what he told himself.

When Sophia was a teen, Elsa was tried, convicted, and died at the hands of a firing squad, though Sophia would have known nothing about that. The ache in him grew as he thought of how that must have been for Elsa. He couldn't even imagine. The grief over her death was sincere and heartfelt, but somehow, not as deep as he imagined it would be.

When he heard of her death, Wesley packed up and flew to Sweden. Once in Malmo he went straight to the private hideaway only he and Elsa knew of, took all of her files, personal journals, and memos, and brought them back with him to the States. It was only then, he discovered the existence of their child and who the adoptive parents were. He'd had no knowledge he'd ever fathered a child, a little girl, until he read Elsa's journals. From the dates in the journals, Wesley read in the journals the baby was adopted without him even knowing of her existence.

Why hadn't Elsa told him of their daughter? When he'd read further he found out her name was Sophia. He had a daughter...and her name was Sophia. Sophia Tennison. He found himself saying the name over and over again. Repeating her name brought with it feelings that surprised him. He liked them. It was akin to having accomplished something really astounding. He could've raised her if Elsa felt it impossible to do on her own. He would've gladly done it. But now, that same daughter would be his undoing. If he'd been the one to raise her, he'd be safe now. There wouldn't have been any flash drive with her name screaming from the file.

Wesley stood and began pacing back and forth, his anger rising with each step. *He* should have been the one to parent her. There were many great boarding schools. She needn't have inconvenienced him in the least, and she'd have wanted for nothing.

By this time, the drive would've been read by any number of people. The news of his double agent status would be common knowledge throughout the Bureau and the NSA by now. The flash drive made Sophia the key to his past and his future. Her life would be the reason for his death.

Wesley had found an entry when he was reading Elsa's journals that startled him. Elsa had a sister and her name was Eve. She'd married an American, they lived in New York City and their last name was Tennison. Unable to have children of their own, Eve and Grainger Tennison decided to adopt. When Elsa heard the news of their desire to have a child, she quickly made arrangements for them to take her baby. An arrangement, which she believed, was in the child's best interest. Thus, Sophia Tennison grew up in the United States.

Eve apparently knew the line of work her sister was in and wanted nothing to do with it. From Elsa's journal he'd learned how Eve despised her sister for what she was doing, but Elsa was still her sister, and so

Eve said nothing, keeping Elsa's line of work a secret. Eve took the child and accepted Sophia as her own.

Elsa apparently cared about the little girl, and tried to follow her life as she grew, at least for a short while. She was usually quite distant from people, not allowing herself to form lasting relationships, except, of course, with Wesley. But he was intrigued by how she'd worked to stay in contact with her sister after the adoption of the baby. He read how it broke her heart when her sister told her to stay away, how she'd mourned for the loss of her child and refused to give up on finding an amicable way to stay in contact with the family. He'd learned how Elsa tracked Sophia's progress and stayed in touch with her sister through various covert means, at least to the extent Eve would allow, which was brief and rare.

As time went by, and again, with the help of the Bureau, he'd discovered there'd been some kind of a rift in the relationship between Sophia and her adoptive parents. When she was seventeen, Sophia wanted to find her birth parents.

At first, Eve and Grainger told Sophia no. Then they decided to soften the blow a little with a lie and tell her the adoption was a closed adoption and neither birth parent wanted to allow contact. The news crushed Sophia, and she refused to believe them. Eve and Grainger couldn't tell her the truth, that her parents were both double agents willing to sell secrets to any country who'd give them the right price. And so the rift was in place, and grew bigger over the years until, as an adult in college, Sophia ceased all contact with her adoptive parents, apparently thinking them insecure and fearful of losing their place in her life to her birth parents, holding to their story that the adoption was closed and they had no control over it.

Several years passed and Wesley fought with himself regarding whether or not he should find Sophia. He loved the thought of having a child, but she was so far removed from his life, it was difficult to know if she would welcome him or hate him for abandoning her. Then he'd have to explain how he hadn't known about her, it was all just so complicated. However, he could continue to watch her from afar. Maybe that would satisfy him.

With the help of his connections at the Bureau, Wesley managed to find her once she graduated college. She was working at an accounting firm in New York City. He watched her; proud of the independent woman she'd grown to be. Then, suddenly, she withdrew from life and he had no idea why. Was she depressed? She'd started looking awful, dark circles under her eyes, barely fixing her hair, her clothes looked unkempt. It wasn't like her. Sophia was usually so fastidious about her appearance.

Wesley wanted to approach her, but he dared not. She was the one link to his double identity, and even *she* wouldn't be worth the jail time. No, he knew she'd have to work this one out on her own, whatever it was.

Imagine his surprise when he discovered her link to Justin Markham. It was then he understood her behavior, more especially, her depression. She was mourning the man she loved, and he could totally understand the heavy sadness he saw in her eyes. It was a tough situation, but life was tough and this was confirmation of that fact. She'd just have to get used to it.

Returning to the present, Wesley surveyed his drab surroundings. The six-drawer dresser was some kind of wood-looking plastic, the walls were in bad need of paint and putty, the carpet felt like it had no pad under it whatsoever, and the bathroom looked like something out of a horror novel.

He pondered his situation as his eyes traveled the room, running several different scenarios in his mind. He contemplated killing Sophia, removing her from the equation, but what possible good would that do? She was, after all, his own flesh and blood, and her death would only draw more attention to him from those who knew of the connection.

Wesley shook his head. The recent fiasco at the warehouse was just what he *didn't* need. He'd barely escaped in the noise and confusion of the takeover. Neo would've seen, though, what good care he'd taken of Sophia as a hostage. Surely he'd be thankful to Wesley for that.

He needed to find a way to retrieve the flash drive, but had no idea who had possession of it now. Finding it would be like looking for a needle in a haystack, but it might be necessary.

His third thought he considered sheer brilliance. If he turned himself into the FBI, demanding a plea bargain, he could avoid the death penalty and get life in prison. With any luck he'd be sent to one of those posh prisons for the mucky mucks. Yeah, that could work in his favor. Maybe he'd make that demand part of his plea bargain. The information he had both in his own files and in what he'd gotten from Elsa's place would ensure acceptance of his demands. Names, dates, places, countries…it was all in there.

He smiled smugly as he crossed his arms over his chest. He could come out of this smelling pretty good if he played his cards right.

Chapter Two

Neo and Sophia sat quietly in a private waiting room. Mrs. Barbosa was waiting outside while the two said their goodbyes.

"Come with me," she whispered. "You're not safe here, Neo. Come with me, please."

Sophia stared hopelessly at her hands in her lap.

"It's safer here for me than it is for you, Sophia," he said, "and neither of us will be safe until this cancer is removed from the FBI and the NSA."

Sophia's pool blue eyes, now filled with tears, stared up at Neo. "What are you not telling me?"

"I'm telling you everything I can."

"No. You're not."

"Sophia, I...you just have to trust me on this."

Sophia lifted his hand and brought it to her mouth, kissing it gently and holding it against her cheek.

"Promise you'll come back to me. Promise me, Neo. I can't leave like this without a promise."

"I promise, Sophia. And when I do come back to you, we won't have to live in hiding anymore. We can go back to our villa on the beach or we can stay in New York. It doesn't matter to me; we can be wherever we want to be."

A small sob escaped her as she turned in her chair, placing both arms around Neo and burying her face in his neck. More sobs escaped with each breath and Neo held her tightly, whispering in her ear.

"Be safe, my love. I'll be home soon, and there'll be no more tears then."

"How can you know that?"

Neo gently took her chin in his hand and lifted her face. He chuckled softly.

"Because, haven't you heard? I'm a savant, and, apparently I know stuff."

Sophia giggled through her tears and took his face in her hands. "You come back safe, or I'll sic Mrs. Barbosa on you."

"That is one threat I will take very seriously." He smiled and kissed her softly on the forehead.

The two stood and walked arm-in-arm to the door. He opened it and saw a red-eyed Mrs. Barbosa who flung her arms around Neo's neck and sobbed.

"You no die. You be safe. I kill you myself if you die." Mrs. Barbosa stepped back, wiping her eyes with a tissue.

"That makes no sense, Mrs. Barbosa, but I'm going to trust you just the same."

"It make perfect sense to me. You come home safe…or else."

A pair of agents approached the three of them.

"It's time to go," said one. "This way please." He motioned for the women to come with them.

Sophia's arms flew around Neo once more and her lips met his with desperate passion. He felt the pain in her kiss, the panic and the need. How could he leave her again? How could this be asked of them *again*?

They were gently pulled apart by one of the agents, their kiss lingering until the last second.

"I'm sorry, ma'am...sir...," said the agent, acknowledging the difficulty of the separation. "We're on a very tight schedule and we really have to leave quickly."

Sophia's eyes remained on Neo as she stepped sideways to keep him in view, half walking, half dragged down the hall and out the door. Mrs. Barbosa followed beside her.

Cayman approached his friend.

"This has to stop," said Neo, staring vacantly at the exit. "I can't keep leaving her like this. I can't live like this."

"It will all be over soon. Hang in there. The love you two have is strong enough that you found each other when you were a whole continent apart. She didn't even know you were you when she saw you in Mukilteo, and yet here you are. I believe there isn't anything that could happen that would keep you two apart for very long." Cayman clapped Neo on the back. "So let's get to it."

Neo heard somewhere the best thing for a broken heart is to keep busy. And Neo was busy from the moment they pulled Sophia from his arms. He refused to allow himself to think about those last painful moments with her. He had to shut them out of his mind because allowing himself to dwell on them even for a moment brought an ache to his gut that made him weak...and he couldn't afford to be weak. He had to keep moving, keep thinking about his work.

Cayman and Neo began by weeding through the interviews of the agents taken at the warehouse.

Neo noticed right away there was one interview missing.

"What about Emmett Matisse?" he asked, rummaging through the stack of papers.

"You won't find him in there, Neo."

"He has to be in here. He was at the warehouse. I shot him myself."

"Yes. Yes you did. But, Neo..." Cayman paused.

"What? Did I kill him? That would be fine with me, because if he'd harmed Sophia in anyway, I would have shot him again as he lay on the ground. I would've-"

"But he didn't, did he? She was far away from the fray, wasn't she? And Mrs. Barbosa was tucked away safely as well. Why do you suppose that was?"

Neo stared at Cayman and a light came on in his head. Cayman saw the look of shock on his face and could almost hear the wheels turning.

"Do you mean...do you mean I shot one of our own? All that time at the mansion he was on *our* side?" Neo was thinking as the words poured from his mouth. "But, he attacked me that day at the zoo in Seattle. He tried to give me a shot and take my memory again."

"But he missed with that syringe, remember?" Cayman gently coaxed the memory from him.

"*I* moved my arm. He would've given me that injection!"

"No, he wouldn't have. He'd have to be beyond dense to think he'd hit your flesh with that needle when it hit dead air. He'd *planned* on missing your arm. You just made it easier for him."

"But, in the car, he said nothing all the way back to the house."

"Your car had an audio bug. You suspected that, remember?"

Neo let the shock settle over him and dissipate. "Do you mean to tell me, he's a double agent? He's *inside* the rogue team?"

"Yes," replied Cayman. "He's our eyes on the inside and when he can, he shoots us lists of those who are connected in anyway with these agents. He just hasn't been able to identify any of those in charge, the ringleaders. Those he sends us are agents and we have to find out if they are willing participants or ignorantly following their superiors, not aware they're working a rogue op."

Neo sat down, collapsing into the chair. "I shot one of the good guys."

"What you did was save his bacon. He looked like one of them, especially when you told me you were actually aiming for his head." Cayman chuckled. "That was a great line, by the way. I'm using that the next chance I get."

Neo grinned weakly. "I think I wanted to talk to Emmett. I wanted him to live so he could tell me how he could allow himself to do the things he'd done to me, to my family, and still look himself in the mirror every day. I really think I may have missed him because I *chose* to miss him, but I'm not sure. Now that we're talking about it, it makes me wonder."

Neo was still struggling with his memory. Desmond had told him it could take up to a year for all his memories to return to normal, and that some of them might not return at all. It was never intended for the serum he'd invented to be used the way the rogue ops team had used it on Neo. He was a guinea pig at this point. Desmond was following his progress from his wheelchair with pencil in hand.

"I want to take a ride over to the warehouse," mused Cayman. "I need to check some things out…satisfy my own curiosity, if you will."

"I'll go with you."

Cayman studied his friend for a moment before speaking. "Neo, I'm not sure being out in the field is a good thing for you just yet. We haven't gotten to the bottom of this rogue op, and there may be some out there that are under orders to terminate you. They may be under the false assumption by doing so, they can save the op, or their own bacon."

"Well, you can't keep me chained to your office for the duration of the investigation. I don't see that as helpful. I may as well have gone with Sophia, if that's the case."

"I know, Neo, but you have to agree with what I'm saying."

"Only if you hold a gun to my head."

"Don't tempt me," Cayman grinned. It was good to see Neo's sense of humor was intact, even if it dripped disappointment.

"Let me ride along," argued Neo. "I'll say in the car and watch the perimeter."

Cayman knew Neo had to be feeling stir crazy. He didn't know how he'd react in the same situation. Neo could take care of himself, and Cayman knew it, so he relented and let him come along.

"So how are the girls?" asked Neo as they waited in traffic. "What did you name them? I can't remember."

"Beautiful, like their mother. They're named after Alexa's two mothers, Max's first and second wife. Elise Rose and Dana Noelle. We call them Rose and Noelle to avoid any confusion." He thought for a minute. "If you and Sophia ever think you want to have twins, think again. What a handful."

"Well, I'm not so sure I have a lot of control over that."

"Yes, you do. Stop having sex…now…before it's too late."

Neo chuckled. "Not gonna happen. I still can't believe you're a daddy to *one* little girl, let alone *two*. Heaven help them both."

Cayman laughed. "Well, at least they look like their mother. They will most likely be just like her. You should hear her father talk about Alexa's tomboy days. Hilarious. And she doesn't appreciate the humor in it. The *only* thing I can see in it is the humor. She pulled a gun on me once, you know."

"After you were married?" Neo was shocked.

"No, before. We didn't know each other very well at that point and I was helping her figure out what really happened to her dad. She didn't know I was FBI, and I couldn't tell her. She's a smart one, and she was sure I wasn't being entirely honest with her, which I wasn't, but, yeah. She pulled a gun on me to get me to 'fess up. It didn't work for her, but it was incredibly *hot*."

They pulled up in front of the warehouse and saw the two guards stationed outside the building both lying on the ground. Neo immediately drew his weapon and crouched down outside the car, scanning the area while Cayman jumped from the car and ran to the agents. They were alive, but out cold, with large bumps on both their temples.

"Now, aren't you glad I came with you?" Neo's eyes continued scanning the surrounding area.

There were crashing sounds from inside the warehouse. Cayman called for backup and an ambulance, then pulled his own weapon and, nodding to Neo and both inched silently into the building.

Chapter Three

Desmond was on the mend and feeling better every day. Ciara was doing a good job playing mother hen and wouldn't let him out of her sight, nor would she let him even *think* about going into the office before the doctor released him for work.

He'd not only been beaten to within an inch of his life, his right leg and right arm were broken along with multiple torn ligaments and tendons in his left leg and a dislocated left shoulder. However, as the weeks moved on, he was becoming tired of keeping tabs on Neo over the phone. He needed to *see* how his vital organs were reacting as the serum made its way out of his body. He needed to know the effects the reduction in serum in his blood stream had, and that would mean physicals and MRI's and CT scans to see how his brain function was doing, none of which he could do from his home. Ciara didn't care a bit and wasn't budging.

"I know you hate being cooped up, but you're staying put. I mean it Desmond. Don't make me call…whoever your boss is now. Cayman. I'll call Cayman if I have to."

"Cayman is not my boss."

"But he'll know who is."

Desmond smiled in spite of his frustration. He was sitting in his wheelchair and Ciara was standing in front of him, arms crossed.

"You're as beautiful as you are stubborn. I'll try not to give you too much grief."

"Yeah, well, they say doctors are the worst patients, and I'm seeing that first hand. Not that I've had many patients in my life, but still…"

"I'm not *that* bad."

"Yes. You are. I'm going to go fix you some lunch."

Desmond watched her saunter away with a satisfied smile on his face. Not that he'd been able to do much about that saunter, but time would take care of that problem.

He turned to the lamp table beside his chair and picked up the note pad he'd used to track Neo's progress and issues. He leafed through the pages slowly, reviewing each one, and decided to call the hospital and set up those MRI and CT scans so he could have the results brought over. If he couldn't do it himself, he'd at least have someone else do it. There were enough notes in his pad to tell him these things needed to be done.

He made the call and set the appointments. He then called Neo and, not getting an answer, left a message on his phone with the appointment time and place.

***

Neo felt the phone on his belt vibrate. *Forgot to turn the ringer back on. Good thing. I really* am *rusty.* He stood beside Cayman just inside the entrance, next to the opening to the hallway. There were more crashes, but they weren't coming from the same room the hostages had been held in. It was a room closer to them.

Cayman peeked around the corner. There were no guards, the door was open and the light was on in the room. He motioned to Neo that the room was clear and to follow him.

They crept down the hallway to the open door. Cayman peeked carefully around the doorframe. He came back around and, leaning against the wall, motioned to Neo there was only one man in the room and for Neo to follow his lead. With guns ready they entered the room.

"Looking for something?" Cayman's voice was even and threatening.

Wesley Tipton turned around slowly with his hands in the air.

"I'm unarmed."

Neo spoke with teeth clenched. "Good, makes it easier to shoot you. Just give me a reason."

Tipton sat down casually in an office chair sitting by itself in front of the boxes he'd been inspecting, the majority of which lay on their sides, open, and empty. There was also an empty file cabinet overturned, obviously the source of all the noise, and several stacked boxes.

"No reason to shoot me. As a matter of fact, I have a bunch of reasons why you shouldn't. I can save you a lot of time interviewing agents and scrutinizing their statements. I can tell you exactly who is involved in this and who isn't. And I can give you more than that if you can meet my demands."

Cayman was obviously ready to shoot the man himself. "You're serious? You have *demands*? You've got a lot of nerve."

"Yes I do, lucky for you. Why don't you just cuff me and take me to your little interrogation room and we'll have a chat. Whaddaya say?"

Neo wasn't sure whether he should spit in his face and *then* shoot him or just shoot him outright.

Cayman reached to the back of his belt and pulled out his handcuffs. As he placed them on Tipton's wrists they clicked into place. After reading him his rights, he continued.

"This arrest implies no guarantee your 'demands' will be accepted, nor does it assume the information you have is worthy of any 'deal.' That will be decided once the information has been reviewed."

The guards were coming around as Cayman and Neo led their prisoner out to the car. Cayman locked Tipton into the backseat and called in the arrest, while Neo checked on the guards.

Neo gently pressed the shoulder of one man back down to the ground. "Stay down, you might have a concussion. We're gonna have paramedics check you out."

"Backup and ambulance are on their way," Cayman called to Neo. "How are they?"

"They're coming around."

It was only a few minutes before they heard the sirens and the ambulance pulled in followed by a black SUV. The backup agents hurried to Cayman, who briefed them on the events and assigned them to guard the warehouse. Whatever information was to be found in the warehouse, if any, would continue to be guarded until it could be removed.

Cayman and Neo started for their vehicle when one of the paramedics approached him.

"We're taking them to the hospital for observation over night. Just wanted to let you know."

"Thank you. Please let them know I'll check in on them later today."

Cayman and Neo entered the SUV to find Wesley watching the guards as the paramedics tended them with a look of amusement.

"You're not fooling anyone by posting those guards, Cayman. There's nothing in there of value."

"What were you looking for then?" Cayman's eyes never left the road.

"We will discuss that at the office. I do suppose you've already seen what's on the flash drive, am I right?"

"Yes, I have, and so has Neo. What of it?"

"Precisely. What of it? What did you get out of the information on there?"

"My job right now, Tipton, is to get you to an interrogation room. What we know or do not know from that drive is not your concern."

There was no response from Tipton and the car fell silent as they returned to Cayman's office. The conversation appeared to have soured Tipton's smugness by a large degree.

Neo radioed ahead for backup to meet them in the parking structure and provide protection for getting Tipton into the building safely.

Tipton smiled bitterly. "No need for more guard dogs. I'm the top of the line. There's no one left to order the hit."

Cayman shook his head. "That doesn't mean someone won't try to kill you to protect their own skin. You know what they say...no honor among thieves."

They pulled into the parking garage and several agents jogged quickly to them. Tipton was escorted in and Cayman pulled Neo back to let some distance grow between themselves and the prisoner. He spoke softly.

"I want you to watch the interview from observation. I think you're too emotionally involved with this man."

This time Neo had to agree. He was emotionally involved. The man had stolen his life and abducted Sophia. Cayman was doing him a favor allowing him to be part of the investigation and he appreciated it.

They continued into the building without incident and left Tipton in the locked interrogation room.

After about an hour, Cayman entered the room and sat down opposite Tipton at the table.

"What were you looking for at the warehouse?"

"Slow down, Agent Richards," said Tipton, leaning forward. "We have a deal to cut, remember?"

"Of all the people who would know how this goes down, you should. In case you've forgotten, however, I'll refresh your memory. You tell me what you've got and I tell you if it's worth whatever you're demanding. Now, what were you looking for at the warehouse?"

"It's in my left front pocket."

Cayman stood and walked to the door. "Agent Green," he called to a man in the corridor, "do you have a minute? I need your assistance in here."

"Sure. What can I do for you?"

"Go to our prisoner's left front pocket and pull out whatever's in there."

Cayman drew his gun and kept it pointed at Tipton. Agent Green walked around the table and pulled out a small key, laying it on the table.

"Thanks for your help, Green."

"You're welcome," he said as he left, closing the door behind him.

"A little dramatic, don't you think?" Tipton was smiling smugly. "You might be wondering why this key was 'missed' in the search."

"I'm a little interested."

"It was well hidden. By me."

"Are you going to tell me what it unlocks or are you going to continue to sit there adoring it?"

"It's a storage room key. I'll give you the address and room number."

"Who else knows about this storage room?"

"No one. This is my personal and private stash of information that will rock your world. No one else knows about it."

Tipton sat back in his chair as Cayman reached into his shirt pocket and pulled out a small notebook and pen. He wrote down the address and storage facility name as it was given him and slipped the notebook back into his shirt pocket. Rising to leave, he stopped at the door as Tipton called to him.

"I'll just be waiting here. Well, in a cell of your choosing, I'm sure. Let me know what you think."

Chapter Four

Leon sat alone in his house, staring out the window and watching the passers by. It was noon and he'd not had breakfast and wasn't hungry for lunch. He knew the toll the beating had taken on him, and he understood PTSD enough to know what was happening to him. He just didn't seem to care enough to do anything about it.

He'd gotten off easy, compared to Desmond Ashler. Leon escaped with no broken bones. However, he had some pretty sore ribs, a concussion and several cuts and bruises. Was he feeling guilty because he wasn't as badly injured as Desmond? He didn't think that was the case, but he had no answers to why he felt so beaten. Surely Desmond was suffering far more than he was. *I'm a therapist. Why can't I identify the problem and move on?*

It was so very nice of Alexa to come and sit with him in the emergency room. Later, Alexa, Cayman and Neo came to the hospital and visited with him. Once he was released, they came every so often to the house for a visit. He appreciated it, but their visits made him question his decision to stay single.

Years ago, when he'd started with the Bureau, he'd thought it unwise to allow his emotions to become tied up with another human being. What kind of life would she have? Neo and Desmond's situations were perfect examples of what could and did go wrong. Leon felt being tied to someone else would make it harder to make the sacrifices many agents make. Would he have gone on this op if he'd had a family to take care of?

But now, sitting by himself and healing by himself, he was rethinking his decision to stay single. It would be nice to have someone to be with right now, someone who would help him if he needed it, empathize with his feelings of isolation and fear. Maybe even someone who would kick him into gear and get him going again when he couldn't make himself do it.

He sighed and watched listlessly as a car pulled up in front of his house. A woman in a smart navy blue business suit exited the vehicle. About his height, she was middle-aged, like he was, and possessed a confident air about her. She pulled a briefcase from the car, straightened her fitted jacket and came around the car, stepping up on the sidewalk with grace. She looked straight at his house and began moving briskly up his front walk.

Who was this woman? A spy sent by the rogue leadership to finish the job? A hit…person? He saw her step onto the porch and he froze. She was going to ring the bell and he couldn't answer it. He wouldn't answer it. But if she'd come to finish the job, he was pretty certain she wouldn't bother to see if he would answer the door. Would she? He'd never had an assassin come to his house before.

The doorbell rang and he froze. *Answer it? Don't answer it? Sit? Stand? Think? Play dead? What am I, a dog in training?* The bell rang again. Footsteps moved to the window and a beautiful woman smiled through the glass at him.

"Mr. Kenning," she began, a little loudly, to be heard through the window, "I'm with the…your employer. I've been assigned to…to help you with some things. May I come in?"

She was quite nice to look at, with large round green eyes, hair like flax that fell softly around an oval face with full lips and white teeth. Pleasant. About his height, she was slender with beautiful skin, like a princess, yes a pr-"

"Mr. Kenning, I need you to open your door. Will you do that for me?"

Leon stood, suddenly aware he was acting like a fool and hurried to the door. He opened it and she stood before him, waiting patiently for him to invite her in.

"Oh, oh, please, come in." He stepped aside and motioned for her to enter, now overly aware of how long it had been since he'd shaved or brushed his teeth, or even combed his hair. He could feel the embarrassment heating his face.

"Thank you. You have a lovely home."

"Just this way, the living room is to your left there." They entered the room and he directed her to a chair, then sat on the couch.

"You've been sent here by the Bureau?"

"Yes, I have," she smiled kindly. "There is…concern…for your emotional well-being. How are you feeling, Mr. Kenning?"

"Leon...call me Leon. I'm, I'm feeling fine, just a little foggy is all."

"Foggy? What does foggy feel like?"

"I can't seem to focus, having a hard time motivating myself. I know the symptoms. It's classic PTSD, but I can't seem to figure out how to get myself back to normal again, whatever *that* is." He smiled weakly.

"That's why I'm here, Leon. I'm going to help you with that."

"You're a psychologist?"

"Psychiatrist. Dr. Rachel Young."

"Ah." Leon stretched out his hand to shake hers. "It's very nice to meet you. I've heard the name, just not had a face to put it with."

The two professionals talked about their work, sharing stories, and before he knew it Leon was actually smiling and feeling human again. It was so refreshing to talk with someone who knew what she was talking about and could relate to the job he did. It was more than refreshing...it was wonderful.

They'd talked for about an hour when Rachel looked at her watch. "Uh-oh. I'm going to be late for an appointment. Would you be interested in meeting again next week?"

Leon smiled and stood. "How about next time we meet over dinner?"

Rachel gazed at him and cocked her head. "You look harmless enough," she said. "I don't usually accept dinner dates from my patients, but I would enjoy dinner with a colleague. Sounds like a plan. Here's my card. Call me and we'll set it up."

He escorted her to the door and they said good-bye. He watched her stride purposefully down the walk, then he shut the door before she could see him watching her.

Leaning against the door, he noticed something suddenly different about himself. What was that he felt? Was that the throbbing of blood pumping through his body, the sound of air filling his lungs? It was the sound of life and it sounded really, really good.

***

Cayman was happy with the direction the investigation was taking. Things were coming along nicely, but he could tell something was bothering his friend.

"What's up?"

Neo adjusted his body in the chair and still looked uncomfortable.

"I can't even *talk* to her, Cayman. I have no idea where she is or if she's okay, how she's doing. I know nothing about her situation and it's killing me. I need her in my life and it's like she's died, only I know she hasn't. At least I *hope* she hasn't, but I have no way of knowing."

Cayman considered Neo. He picked up his cell phone and paused, glancing at Neo one more time before dialing.

"Hey. I need a favor."

There was silence as Cayman listened to the speaker on the other end of the line.

"Yes, I'll fill this end in on that and you take care of your end. Tell me when you're ready."

Cayman flashed Neo a warning look. He covered the speaker on his cell phone before speaking.

"No names, no dates, no places. Nothing. You're calling to hear her voice and she yours. It has to be short and sweet, but it's at least something."

Neo's eyes brightened and he took the phone when Cayman handed it to him. Before releasing it, Cayman gave Neo another warning look. "Absolutely *no* names."

Neo gave him a hurried nod and took the phone.

When he heard Sophia's voice Neo had to force himself to not say her name. He'd not understood how difficult that part would be.

"I'm here," he said. "I can't tell you how good it is to hear your voice."

"And yours," she said. He could hear her tears, "...and yours."

"Just tell me you're doing fine and I'll be happy."

"I'm missing you, but I'm safe. I'm so happy to hear from you."

"I will see you soon. Very soon."

"I love you." Their voices spoke in unison as the line went dead.

"That was a bit abrupt." Neo handed the phone back to Cayman.

"The call itself was a risk, but necessary. She's been having as hard a time as you have. The phone he has is untraceable as far as we know, but you know how that works. We have to be vigilant."

Cayman picked up the key he'd gotten from Tipton's shirt pocket. "I wonder what secrets we'll really find answers for, and how much of those 'secrets' we already know. Tipton appears to have lost his grip on reality to some extent. I wonder if he thinks he's got more than he actually has."

"I know him. I've worked with him before." Neo shifted gears and worked to once again focus on the task at hand. He was trying to hang on to the euphoria of her voice, but the sadness in her tears made him ache inside. He forced himself to focus on the fact she was safe, and doing well. That's all that mattered.

"And...?" Cayman's voice brought him back to the present.

"Oh, yeah, and he was always a good guy, a runner, if I remember correctly. He seemed pretty together to me. I just wonder if getting caught with his pants down has thrown him off his game. It has to, don't you think?"

"Yes, I'm sure, but what's your point?"

"Well...I'm not so sure he's lost it, I think it's more about trying to *act* like he's lost it. You can't live the life he's lived for the past however many years, keep it from the U.S. Government and all your associates and not have your story tied up pretty tight. He is fully aware of what he's doing, and I'm betting he has an angle. Has he said what his demands are? What kind of a deal he wants to make?"

"No, I made him tell me what he had to offer first and if we found it useful he could list his demands with me."

"Well, then I think we should get to it and see if he has anything useful."

Cayman flipped the key into the air, catching it again. "That sounds like a plan."

The men were in the car in minutes and on their way to the address on Cayman's notepad. It wasn't a long drive and there was no issues getting into the storage facility with the unit number he was given. Within a half an hour they were standing in front of the storage unit door.

"What do you say we bet? I say he's bluffing." Cayman was grinning that surfer- boy smile, his eyes twinkling with mischief.

"No, he's not bluffing. He's as serious as a heart attack. I say there is a gold mine behind that door." Neo stretched his back, bringing his height up to its full 6'5" frame. "Yeah," he said, running his hands through his, once again, sandy brown hair. "He's dead serious."

Cayman started laughing. "You have the lousiest poker face I think I've ever seen." He stuck the key in the padlock and turned it until the shackle dropped. He slowly raised the large aluminum door. What they saw brought a low whistle from Neo and a gasp from Cayman. "You win," whispered Cayman in awe.

Paper bills in large denominations lined the left wall from floor to ceiling with what looked like trip wires surrounding them. Along the back and right walls were boxes stacked upon boxes. They looked like they'd been hurriedly placed, almost dumped in the unit. Although that was the most important part of the stash, the men couldn't help but stare at the 'money wall.'

Neo followed the wires to the source of the charge and disconnected it. They carefully examined the rest of the unit to make sure there were no other wires or set charges.

"Interesting he never told us about the booby traps," mused Neo as he studied the remainder of the unit."

"For sure." Cayman smiled smugly. "I fear that's going to come back to bite him in the butt when it comes to his bargaining ability."

When the men were certain all the traps had been discovered and dismantled, they radioed the office and ordered a small moving van brought to the warehouse. The information would have to be reviewed at the Bureau where it was more secure. Not forgetting the fact that there was just something about standing beside millions of dollars in currency that made them both a little uneasy.

Chapter Five

The boxes and cash were loaded into a moving van and whisked to the FBI office. A quick look into a few of the boxes revealed the contents to have been written by one Elsa Lindgren. If all the boxes contained similar information, the information alone would be worth more than the money that lined the opposite wall.

The CIA was invited to be part of the team that read and recorded what was in the boxes. The money was put in the FBI safe until they could discuss what should be done with it. The most important thing was translating and categorizing the information in what was now known as the Lindgren Papers.

An oversized conference room was set up with long tables lengthwise down opposite sides of the room. On one side the tables had workstations set up with powerful computers, and on the other side, the tables held high-speed scanners at each station. Agents on this side of the room scanned documents from boxes taken from the storage unit and put them in computer files. The agents on the other side extracted the files, then translated and categorized the scanned images.

Several multi-lingual agents poured over the papers, books and logs, presorting them for the scanners. Other multi-lingual agents translated the scanned files. As quickly as a page was translated and deciphered (if necessary), it was transferred to another set of agents who extracted the intelligence information from each page.

As lists were compiled from the data, names flew onto screens like bees to a hive as the translators worked. There were many names, some known, some unknown, but one name, one very dangerous name, hit several screens at the same time and the room quieted instantly.

Tristan Bradford was the current Deputy Director of Security at the NSA and as such had his finger into the investigations of new technologies especially pertinent to daily operations of the NSA. The date on this specific document made reference to his early days with the Agency. No one would ever have suspected Bradford of setting up a rogue operation capable of doing what was done to Neo, but from the look of the documents they now saw before them, he was the ringmaster. Neo's and Desmond's discoveries would've been right up there on that list of new technologies. Valuable beyond anything imaginable, Tristan apparently decided to sell Neo's information to the highest bidder. But in order to obtain the algorithm locked in Justin Markham's brain, Tristan concocted a plan that would destroy several lives. Motivated only by greed, he set his plan in motion.

The initial reason for bringing Neo in to infiltrate the rogue group was the amount of information that had either gone missing, or had been 'leaked' to other countries. The 'loss of Justin Markham' had definitely slowed the mission. Still, no one had ever questioned the loyalty of Tristan Bradford, nor would they ever have thought his name would show up on a computer screen of information provided by a mercenary agent such as Elsa Lindgren. He'd been the one to suggest using Justin Markham to infiltrate the rogue operation. He'd been the one to notify both the NSA and the FBI of Justin's death. The shockwave roared silently through the group.

Permission to perform an op such as the one that 'killed' Justin and used the serum made by Desmond Ashler would have had to come from someone high up in the structure of either the NSA or the FBI. Even though Tipton intimated he was the top of the food chain on this op, it was now clear he was protecting Tristan Bradford. Still, all the information they were retrieving had to be backed up with fact, and that was going to take time.

Cayman stopped what he was doing and addressed the group. "Listen up. You all know that you've been cleared for this operation. You've been briefed on the types of things you may see as you look at these papers. The information you see doesn't leave this room. I know I don't have to say that, but I just want to make it perfectly clear. There are only twenty-five of us here. If there is a leak among us, it won't be hard to find. Now, let's get back to it."

The soft murmurs started once again as information was passed to those entering the decrypted or translated pages into the computer system. It was a tedious process, but necessary.

Everyone entering or leaving the secured room was searched and visually scanned. This information had to be protected. If they were going to investigate the leads they got from the pages, those investigations had to be a surprise.

***

Tipton was led into the interrogation room, seemingly happy to be there. He greeted both Neo and Cayman with polite salutations and took his seat at the table, talking as he was led slowly because of the shackles on his hands and feet. He paid no attention to the restraints, other than being careful not to fall.

"It's good to see you boys. How is the investigation going? Did I not tell you the information I had was incredibly valuable? Are you making good use of it?"

Neo was seething inside. What this man had done to him, to his family, was unthinkable, and here he sat, making cordial conversation as if nothing had happened. Cayman gave him a warning nod. Unable to contain himself, Neo stood, shoving the chair away from the table with his legs and strode quickly to the door.

"I don't want to be in the same room as this…" he didn't finish his sentence, but left the interrogation room. He was surprised he'd lasted as long as he had. Neo went into the observation room. That was as close as he dared get.

Tipton was sitting back in his chair, talking amicably with Cayman. "That is one talented kid. He can do the work of five agents. Five *well-trained* agents. I admire him."

"Interesting you could say such a thing," mused Cayman, "since you stole his life, killed his family and abducted him illegally. How do you reconcile that?"

Tipton smiled, a reminiscent kind of smile. "It was for the good of the Agency, you see. He was willing to help, and we knew he would be fine with the op as it went down. Sure, there were adjustments that had to be made, but we were certain he would be accepting of those things."

Cayman was stunned. He couldn't believe what he was hearing. "So, what you're saying is the murder of three innocents, Neo's family to be specific, was an 'adjustment' to the operation? A simple adjustment you were certain he'd be 'accepting of?'"

"Well, yes, it was. I'm not sure I understand your surprise."

Cayman stood, a sudden realization hitting his senses. "You'll excuse me for a minute?" Without waiting for a reply, Cayman turned and left the room.

He entered the interrogation room to see a furious Neo pacing back and forth; doing his best to maintain some sense of decorum.

Cayman spoke first. "Okay, so there are only three explanations here that are possible. The first is he's pretending to be crazy to avoid the death penalty, second, he's sheer evil, or third, he's not pretending and is completely off-his-rocker insane."

Neo scoffed. "I choose door number two, with maybe a little paint scraped off of door number one. No one has that level of insanity and hides it for so many years. He's a coward who's out to protect himself. He knows exactly what it takes to sound crazy."

"He needs to be assessed by a psychiatrist. I'll have to call and set that up. Sometimes these things are triggered by an event that suddenly sets them off. I'm no counselor, but something is very strange about this." Cayman studied his friend. "Are you going to be okay?"

"Yeah, I'm sure I will be. I worry about Sophia and Mrs. Barbosa every day, then this moron comes in and does his phony little dance...I just want to find a quiet place to be with Sophia and let the rest of the world go. I don't want to be here anymore. I'm done with the FBI, the NSA and the CIA. Done."

"You still have a lot of good that you can do, Neo, but I wouldn't blame you one bit for walking away. Just give it some time before you make a decision. This is a lot to digest in one sitting. Let it ride for a while. In reality, no one is going to feel as much pain as you do at the loss of your family. If Tipton ever was a good guy, that good is long gone."

Cayman knew it was imperative he get Neo busy right away.

"We've got to organize at least three teams. As the investigation goes on, we may need more. Every name on that list has to be investigated, covertly. No one can know they're being looked at. Are you up for heading a team?"

Neo eyed his friend. "I know what you're doing, and you're right for doing it. I need to be busy. Yes, I'll head a team, but we get the privilege of investigating Tipton and Bradford."

"I'll give you that," said Cayman. "You deserve more, but if you can bring these guys down, maybe you'll get some kind of closure."

Neo nodded and headed for the door.

"Neo," called Cayman. He stopped with his hand on the doorknob and turned to face his friend. "Be careful. We only have Tipton and we don't know how many are out there looking for you. I'll work on your team, if you don't mind. You're in my charge until we know you're safe."

Neo said nothing but nodded and left the room. He closed the door behind him and headed to the break room. He needed some coffee, with a shot of something much stronger, if he could find it...and he needed to shoot something. Maybe a trip to the shooting range would be in order.

Arriving at the break room, he poured himself a cup of what looked more like mud than coffee. He sat down at the table and remembered he'd not checked the messages on his phone for a couple of days. Only two people had his number or even knew he had a cell phone - Desmond and Cayman. Even Sophia didn't know, for her own safety. She had another number to call in case of an emergency.

As Neo checked his messages he found several calls and messages from Desmond. He started at the first one and by the time he got to the fifth message he realized he wasn't going to be able to wrangle his way out of a trip to the hospital for the required scans.

He took a drink of coffee and quickly spit it back into the cup. It was awful, barely warm. After dumping the contents of the cup into the sink, he rinsed it out and set it on the counter. He needed to find Cayman. Maybe Cayman could help him find an excuse to get out of the hospital trip.

Finding his friend did him no good at all. In less than an hour, Neo and Cayman were on their way to the facility where the scans would be done.

"You're way too busy for this babysitting errand," spat Neo. "And I need to get my team organized and get moving on this investigation. This is a waste of time."

"One hour isn't going to make a difference one way or another. You just don't want to do the scan. It's important to Desmond's study that he see how your body reacts to the gradual loss of the serum in your system. And truthfully, the Bureau needs to know you're okay as well. You know that's true."

"Complete waste of time." Neo's frown made Cayman chuckle. He was glad he didn't have to be in the same room with Neo for the scans. Cayman was happy to wait in the waiting area.

Chapter Six

Cayman was ushered into the waiting area, just as he'd thought. He wasn't much good at the waiting game and soon began to feel uncomfortable. Neo had been in the imaging department for about thirty minutes and Cayman's gut was telling him something wasn't right. He stood and paced for a couple minutes before approaching the nurse's station.

"Can you tell me what exam room Neo Weston is in?"

"I'm sorry sir, you can't go back there," replied the nurse patiently. "You'll have to stay in the waiting area."

Cayman's frustration level was rising. He *knew* something wasn't right. Pulling out his badge he held it up for the nurse to read. "I need to get into that room, right now."

Her eyes widened and she stepped around the station to take him back to the exam room.

***

Neo put the loose and somewhat revealing gown on, complaining softly to himself every minute. The attendant came back and ushered him into the room where the scan would be done. Neo was directed to sit on a cold hard table and the process was explained to him in some detail.

Less talk, more scan. I need to get out of here.

Neo lay down on the table attached to the scanner and the attendant secured his arms to his side with a pair of soft cuffs and his feet to the table with the same type of cuffs.

"These are just to keep you from moving. You'll have to lie very still during the scan."

Having never had a scan before, Neo didn't think it too odd to be restrained, but there was a nagging concern in his head. *This is a hospital. I'm safe here. It'll be fine.*

The room became very quiet as the attendant finished the preparations for the scan. He turned away from the table when suddenly a man in a surgical mask, gown and cap came up behind him and hit him on the head and Neo watched the attendant sink to the floor as he pulled and wrestled impotently against the restraints.

The assailant pulled a small vial and a syringe from his pocket and slowly removed the cover from the needle. With the precision of a physician, the assailant began filling the syringe with the contents of the vial. He tapped the syringe with his finger to remove the bubbles and looked down at Neo.

Neo was struggling to get out of the restraints, but it was no use. He was held fast and couldn't move.

"No! No! I won't do this again!" Neo was yelling as loudly as he could, but no one came. "Stop him! Stop him! He's not a hospital employee!"

The man moved the sleeve of the hospital gown from Neo's arm as Neo continued to struggle against the restraints, yelling as loudly as he could.

Suddenly the door opened and the nurse who'd escorted Cayman was moved quickly out of the way as Cayman rushed to Neo's aid.

The assailant turned at the noise and Cayman slammed his fist into the man's face. He stumbled back against the table as Cayman hit him again and the syringe flew from his hand, bouncing off the wall and landing on the floor, the vial landing not far from the syringe. The man began to fight back, landing a solid blow to Cayman and shoving him against the wall. Cayman's head hit the wall and he slid to the floor, stars dancing before his eyes. The nurse pushed the emergency button while the two men fought and Neo's attacker knew he had no time to complete his assignment. He ran to the door and down the hall. Cayman struggled to his feet.

"Get him off that table," he said hoarsely, pointing to Neo. He ran out the door but the man was gone. Hospital security was running toward the imaging room. "He's gone," said Cayman, to the men. "I have no idea which way he ran. He wore a surgical gown and a mask over his face."

Cayman hurried back to the room where Neo was just sliding off the table. "Now do you see why I won't let you out of my sight? I should've been in here with you. They almost had you again."

Neo leaned against the table, feeling a little weak in the knees. The weakness didn't last long before the fury set in. He was so angry that he was still dealing with this, but thankful at the same time knowing Sophia and Mrs. Barbosa were safe.

Neo changed into his clothes while Cayman waited outside the dressing area. Both men were a little on edge and Cayman wanted to get Neo back to the Bureau as quickly as he could. There were people out there still after him, and even worse, they were brazen enough to attempt an abduction in a hospital. That means they were desperate.

Unable to stop thinking about it, Neo wondered as he dressed why they would think the rogue op could still be going with one of the main leaders in custody. But, his assumption was that the syringe they tried to inject him with had Desmond's serum in it. What if it was something else? What else? Did they want him dead if they couldn't control the code in his head?

He finished dressing and hurried out to Cayman.

"What if they weren't trying to erase my memory, Cayman? What if they were trying to kill me?"

"What would be the point of that?"

"These guys have to be into some major computer hacking. If they had the code, they could control the hacking. If they didn't have the code, they would be locked out of every system they are currently skimming money from, or hijacking information from. My algorithm could ruin their livelihoods."

Cayman whistled low and long. "That changes everything. The contents of that syringe will be identified. Once we know what it is, that will answer a lot of questions for us. But you may be in more trouble that we originally thought."

Neo shook his head slowly. "Just seems like I can't catch a break around here. I wish I'd never seen that code in my head. Really wish I'd never seen it."

They drove back to Cayman's office at the FBI. Cayman couldn't think of a thing to help Neo. However, one idea did pop out.

"You know, since you still have that code, you could be filthy rich if you sold it to the government."

"I'm already filthy rich. A lot of good that's done me."

"Oh, yeah, forgot about that. Sorry."

"You're good, Cayman. I just can't believe it's come to this. And it's not just me I have to think about now. I have Sophia and Mrs. Barbosa. They have to be protected as well. The more I think this nightmare is about over, the worse it gets. I'm just really frustrated right now. I need to see my wife, I need to hold her in my arms and know that she is safe."

"Think about what you're saying, Neo. You want to bring her back to the fray? Look what just happened to you! What if they'd succeeded? What if they found out Sophia or even Mrs. Barbosa was back here and used them to get to you? It's just not safe for any of you around here. You're only here because you have a unique perspective on this op. Not to mention your skills as a sniper, cryptographer and agent. We need you on this one, Neo. We really do."

There it was again. That hinge thing again that kept everything moving. It exhausted him, to always be the one person everyone needed. He just wanted to have a life. He wanted to *live* that life. He stared out the window at all the people walking by who knew nothing of his struggle, people who were just living and breathing and going about their day. He sighed, realizing for the first time just how much he envied them.

Sometimes he wanted to scream at the inequality of life. But other times, he found himself immensely grateful for the opportunities he'd been given to help the people of his country and often, to aid in helping other countries. It was an honor that he could not deny. That didn't always make it any easier, but it helped.

At this point in his life, with the loss of his family and his separation from Sophia, he was at the breaking point again. He'd get through this, he always did, but it was becoming more and more difficult as his time away from Sophia increased. He knew it was important to finish this, to see it through to the end. And he would do that. But once this rogue op was cleaned up, he would never be separated from Sophia again. Ever.

"What are you thinking about so hard over there?" Cayman's eyebrows furrowed, his face in a half smile, half frown.

"Nothing really, and everything."

Cayman pulled the car onto the side of the road a few blocks from the parking structure and Neo, his mind elsewhere, started to get out of the car.

"Whoa, Neo. We're going to wait for the backup to check out the parking garage. We want to make sure we're not walking into an ambush."

"When did you call for backup?"

"While you were in lala land somewhere."

"You know, Cayman, if you want to sit here and let backup agents put their lives on the line to save my butt, go right ahead. But if you're really expecting an ambush in there, then I'm going in with the backup.
"

Neo pulled his sidearm out and checked his ammo, grabbed a few extra clips from the glove box and shoved them into his pocket. He glanced sideways at his 'body guard' and saw he was doing the same thing.

"Okay, fine," grumbled Cayman. "But for the record, this is a terrible idea."

Keeping behind cars parked at the curb, Neo and Cayman made their way on foot to the parking garage and entered via the rear pedestrian entrance. Cayman tried to make contact with the backup team, but they must have been in the elevator on the way down.

Cayman and Neo took up positions by the emergency stairwell with guns drawn and scanned the area.

"There's someone here, all right," muttered Neo, his eyes never leaving the garage. "I can smell 'em."

"You can *smell* them?"

"Yeah, I can smell their guns, the leather in their holsters."

"How do you know you're not smelling *our* guns and holsters?"

Neo smiled slyly. "Because my gun smells better than theirs do."

Cayman scoffed and shook his head. Just as they finished their conversation, four agents exited the elevator with guns drawn. They scanned the area checking for threats. Within seconds of their exiting the elevator, the air was filled with gunfire and two agents went down. Neo took cover behind the car next to them and quickly but silently made his way to a place that gave him a better view of where the gunfire was coming from.

He found the shooters, hidden in the upper level that overlooked the level his team was on. They were nearly invisible. Neo raised his gun, slowed his breathing, found the first shooter, making note in his head where the second shooter was in relation to the first. He squeezed the trigger twice, killing both shooters. Cayman ran to check his men with Neo right behind him. The men were hurt, but not dead. Cayman radioed for an ambulance and ordered Neo into the building while he waited with the injured men and the other two agents swept the parking garage. Neo understood the necessity of getting out of the line of fire, but he felt like a coward running from a fight. He knew his being there would only put every other agent in jeopardy. One day…one day there would be no more hiding.

Chapter Seven

Desmond answered the call and listened intently, his concern growing with each word from the cell phone. When he ended the call he stared up into the beautiful oval face of Ciara. Her creamy black skin glistened in the morning sun, her eyes huge with worry.

"What, Desmond? What's happened?"

"There was an attempt on Neo again. It's unclear whether they were trying to take him again or kill him. They won't know which until the substance in the syringe they tried to use on him is identified."

"Oh, no." Ciara sat down in the chair across from Desmond. "This is a terrifyingly clear picture of what greed does."

Desmond considered the fear in her eyes. "I'm certainly worried for Neo, and glad that Sophia is in protective custody. However, those in charge of this rogue op are still out there, and they are aware of you, of me, and of my relationship with Neo. They may even know by now I was the one who hid Neo, Sophia and Mrs. Barbosa away the first time. We could be in danger as well."

The phone rang again and it was Cayman. "Mind if I come by? We have some things to discuss."

Desmond smiled softly. "I'm pretty sure it's the same 'things' Ciara and I were just talking about."

"I'll see you in thirty minutes."

The call ended and Desmond returned to his conversation with Ciara. "That was Cayman. He's on his way over."

Ciara bowed her head, her shoulders slumped, and she began to cry.

"Come over here," he said softly, holding out his good arm. "Why the tears, Ciara?"

She stood and walked to him, kneeling down beside him and resting her head on his shoulder. "I'm so proud of you for doing what you did for Neo. I know that took enormous courage. I just want to have that same courage now, for you, to help where I can and do what I can. It's just that, I feel so frightened, and how can I be strong and frightened at the same time?"

Desmond squeezed her gently. "When this is over, I'm going to marry you, if you'll have me. And then I'm going to take you on a honeymoon you'll never forget. As for the frightened part, you ask anyone who's ever prepped for a fight and they'll be the first to tell you there is no courage without fear. Fear is the piece that keeps you from doing stupid things; it's the piece that enables the courage."

He lifted her chin and kissed her softly. Her lips were soft, warm, and he could feel her strength returning as the fire smoldered inside them. Ciara's kiss told him everything he needed to know…but could do nothing about. He cursed the casts that covered pretty much the whole right side of his body.

"We're going to have an incredible time on that honeymoon."

Ciara giggled softly and kissed his forehead. "Let me see if I'm hearing you correctly. You're going to marry me, take me on a honeymoon and show me what fear really is. Did I get it all?"

Desmond roared with laughter as Ciara stood. "You're amazing. You really are."

Ciara knelt down again and smiled that smoldering smile. "You are all talk, Mr. Ashler. Why don't you just shuck off those casts and come and get me?"

"Oh you think you're all that, don't you? Well, I haven't heard you tell me if you're going to marry me or not. Why would I risk further injury when you may be playing me."

"Hmmm…I *definitely* wouldn't want to 'risk further injury.' I need you healthy as soon as possible," Ciara ran her hands over his muscled stomach and grinned broadly. "So, if I'm hearing you correctly, and I think I am, you want an answer now. Shouldn't I have a week to think that over? It's a big step, you know."

"I want you to be my wife." Desmond pulled her into his good arm and laid her gingerly across his lap. "If I have to secure you to the outside of the plane with rope, we *will* be married and we *will* have that honeymoon."

"You make it sound so…romantic. How could a woman refuse a proposal such as that? I'm telling your mom."

The doorbell rang and Ciara went to answer it. It was Cayman and Neo, and Desmond was happy to see them both.

"You're lucky," grinned Neo. "That black skin hides most of the bruising, but if I look close enough I can see it."

Desmond moved his head away from Neo who was bent over inspecting his face. "Just keep your distance. You know how rumor travels in the Bureau."

Neo chuckled. "Seriously, you look great. How much longer in the chair?"

Desmond looked forlornly at his casted right side. "Not really sure. With casted arm and leg on the right, crutches are currently out of the question. But as soon as I'm given the go-ahead, I'm outta this thing. It's driving me crazy. I think my butt's been asleep for three weeks, at least."

"Yeah, well, just don't push it too fast," warned Cayman. "We want you back strong and healthy."

Neo and Cayman sat on the couch. Ciara stood. "Can I get you something to drink…some coffee?"

"That sounds great, if it's not too much work." Cayman smiled up at her.

"Not at all. How about you, Neo?"

"I'll take some, as well. Thanks, Ciara."

When she left the room, Cayman began explaining their concerns, speaking softly.

"Desmond, this last attack on Neo makes us concerned for your safety, and that of Ciara. I think at the very least we need to get a protection detail assigned to your home, day and night."

"Ciara is very aware of the danger," said Desmond. "She and I were talking before you called. She gets the connection, so don't worry about frightening her. She's scared, but she's also very strong."

"We just want to protect you both. With you stuck in that chair for a while longer, it would be very hard to get you out of the house in a hurry, should the need arise. Talk it over with Ciara. We can put you someplace safe and we're happy to do it. You'll have to decide quickly, we should move you today if at all possible."

Ciara returned with the coffee and Desmond put the question of staying or going into protective custody to her. Her relief at the words 'protective custody' was apparent. She looked as if her whole body relaxed.

"Protective custody, please. I worry so much about Desmond and how to keep him safe. I wouldn't know what to do if someone came here and tried to take us. Protective custody sounds great."

Desmond so wanted her at that moment. It was all he could do to keep himself in the wheelchair. The only thought that kept him where he was, was the image of having his friends peel him off the floor and put him back in the chair. There was just something about humiliation that completely destroyed a mood.

"Here I am worried about you, and you're worrying about me," Desmond said, smiling up at Ciara. "Let's go pack up some things." He turned to Cayman and Neo, "If you're ready, you can take us with you when you go."

"That works for us." Neo, too, was relieved by the decision. "We'll make some calls and get it arranged while you pack."

It took the two of them about thirty minutes to throw some things into a bag. Neo assured them if they forgot something he'd be happy to pick anything up at the store the might need.

Within the hour they were in the car, Desmond's chair was folded and in the trunk with two bags between him and Ciara on the back seat. He smiled at his future wife; happy to see the burden she'd felt taken from her shoulders. It bothered him that she had to be in this mess with him, and how much it had stressed her. He'd not realized how much weight she'd carried. He felt guilty for that and swore to himself he'd never put her in this position again.

Their new home was going to be a nice hotel in downtown D.C., close to the Hoover building with only one entrance into their third floor room. Cayman insisted on adjoining rooms for the protection detail, four agents there all the time, two men on duty and two men off duty and sleeping. The on duty agents would monitor the door from the computers inside the adjoining room. This would make their room number less conspicuous.

Within an hour they were at the hotel, checked in and settling into their surroundings. The room had a living room with full kitchen and two bedrooms, each with its own bath. Agents were posted outside in the hallway.

As Cayman and Neo drove back to the office, they discussed a plan for capturing anyone who might try to get to Desmond and Ciara. Neo suggested video equipment to monitor anyone coming to the door. With agents posted outside the door, it was obvious which room Desmond and Ciara were in. He felt it would be better if the agents watched the door from inside the adjoining room. Cayman radioed the office and made those arrangements while Neo drove them back to the office.

After receiving radio confirmation of an 'all-clear' from agents Cayman had guarding the garage, Neo pulled in and parked the car as close to the elevators as possible. Exiting the car quickly, they made their way to Cayman's office.

Computer equipment was ordered and brought to the room next to Desmond's via the utility elevator. With as many people as they had working on the project, it took less than three hours to get the job done. The agents took up residency in the room as soon as the work was complete. All that was left to do was to wait and see if anyone came calling.

***

The contents of the syringe were found to be the same serum used to wipe Justin Markham's memory. The assailant was never found and the trail went dead, except for the serum. The batch was identified by the number off the vial and was traced to a requisition order. That order was signed, neatly and efficiently by none other than Tristan Bradford. But another name was also on the purchase order. Raymond Mathens was the deliveryman. Mathens picked up the case of twelve vials and delivered them to Bradford.

The fact that the pickup and delivery of the serum was done by Agency employees was suspect, but not so much so that it would be used as evidence. Neither of the signatures was strong enough evidence of wrong-doing to effect an arrest of either man. However, they were pieces to a larger picture that, one day, would allow for a search warrant, and eventually, an arrest warrant.

Chapter Eight

Leon held the dining chair for Rachel as she slid gracefully into it and sat down. He walked to his seat and sat down across from her, smiling at the beauty that now graced his table.

The waiter came to take their drink order.

"We'll have a bottle of your best Cabernet, please."

"Yes, sir. Right away."

The waiter left their table and Leon smiled at his guest.

"I'm happy we could have dinner. It's always nice to see you." He could see the concern on her face and knew what she was going to say before she said it.

"Leon…" Rachel hesitated. "I'm not sure this is a good idea. We're colleagues, yes, but you're also my patient. I shouldn't be romantically involved with a patient. You, of all people, should know that."

"We can fix that right now," smiled Leon. "I'm firing you. You're no longer my therapist. There, how's that?"

"It would be perfect, except that the Bureau hired me, not you, and it's the Bureau that says when I'm done working with you, upon my recommendation."

Leon considered her words. "Well, what do you think? Am I ready to return to work? I feel great; I'm even shaving and showering every day." He smiled slyly, teasing her, yet still hearing the truth in her logic.

"Leon, I...I just wonder how you would be feeling now if I weren't in the picture. You and I both need to know that you're back to your old self whether I'm in the picture or not. I think we need to stop seeing each other and see how you do. This is important, Leon."

He could feel his heart sinking. "You're right of course. It only makes sense."

They'd not been seeing each other for that long, but the few weeks they'd been together filled a place in his heart that had never been filled. In fact, Leon hadn't even known it was empty. Now that he'd had his first real chance to open up that private place, there was no turning back. Oh, he'd dated. He'd dated plenty. But he realized now he'd closed himself off to his own need for love and companionship, so he'd not seen it when it was standing right in front of him, until now. He knew that now, and he also knew that often a traumatic event would trigger the opening of those doors. That's exactly what had happened in Leon's case. His own training could explain what was happening to him, but his heart would have him skip over the fine points of his recovery and move right on to a relationship. He was aware of the tenuous nature of such a move, but he also knew none of the other women he'd dated was the right combination of smart, sexy and beautiful that he'd found in Rachel.

Rachel began speaking again, snapping him back to the present.

"I need to assess how you'll do if I'm not seeing you on a personal basis any longer. Will you still be able to function or will you go back to the way you were that first day we met?"

The waiter brought the wine as Rachel stood to go. "I'm sorry, Leon, but it's best to tear the bandage off quickly." She nodded to Leon and turned, moving gracefully between the tables.

He felt the doors on his heart begin to close, felt the emptiness of the place there and fought to keep the loneliness and sadness from filling him. Could he go on? Could he continue his work and show himself that he was ready to move ahead, alone if need be?

"Cancel the wine," said Leon softly, "and cancel the reservation." He left the dining room, getting to the street as Rachel was entering a taxi. Leon hailed the next taxi and gave the driver his home address. She was right of course.

The psychiatrist in him knew the truth, but the deeper truth was that he'd found himself again. He could see clearly through the pain of the torture they'd put him through. He understood what it had done to his psyche, the depression and fear it caused in him and he understood why it affected him the way it did.

But the real truth lay in the pain he felt when there was no one to call in case of an emergency, when there was no one to notify of his condition. No one came to visit him at the hospital, except of course his associates and friends from the workplace, but no family, no one special in his heart. He was alone in the world, and for the first time in his life, Leon knew he'd made a wrong decision in staying single. The plan he'd written for his life was grossly flawed.

But now he had to ask himself the one question he'd never had to ask before. Was he relying on Rachel for the strength she possessed, or had he really found himself again? These were questions that could only be answered in time, and time was something he had plenty of.

***

With an interim report from Rachel, Leon was back at his desk for half days. He was itching to be back full-time, but he was aware of the effects of post traumatic stress, and the powers that be wanted to make sure he was not having issues with that.

Seeing Rachel at work was more difficult than he'd thought it would be. But he had to realize that she might not be coming back into his life. She was distant, and professional, yet she was kind and pleasant. She was moving on and he could see it. Funny, though, how it was okay with him. He understood how these things worked, with one difference. He *was* going to start dating. He was going to find someone he could build a life with. Maybe that person was Rachel…he certainly hoped it was, but for now she would be just a colleague. The small voice in the back of his head told him any relationship he made needed to be on his terms, not on the terms of the lonely, frightened man he'd almost become. He was more than ready to move on, to return to the man he was before his kidnapping. In spite of the sadness he felt every now and then, he felt stronger.

For now, Leon carried a light client load and was able to focus on their issues and keep his own in check. Everything was going well and Cayman called and asked Leon if he was ready to give his report of the events leading up to and including the abduction of Justin Markham. They met at the Hoover building in a secure conference room.

"You know, Leon," said Neo, settling in to his seat at the table. "I've been wanting to hear your version of our experience in Mukilteo."

"I was thinking you might want to do that at some point."

Without wasting any time, Neo jumped right in.

"Who was your contact there? Who was it you reported to?"

"My immediate supervisor was Tristan Bradford. I spoke on the phone with someone after each one of your appointments, and but I was never given that persons identity. Sometimes it sounded like Bradford, but most of the time I couldn't tell for sure."

"What were Bradford's specific instructions?"

"Well, I can only speak for myself, but basically it was to help Neo Weston, whom I'd not met before, work through his accident and come to grips with his memory loss. The therapy would require relocation to the west coast, as they wanted the agent to be far removed from any trauma that could cause him issues with recovering his memory. At least, that was how it was presented initially. I actually asked them why they didn't go with a local therapist out west and they insisted I was perfect for the job because of my single, unattached status and my 'expertise' in my field."

"When did your feelings begin to change in reference to the op?" Neo was still the one asking the questions.

"There were little things, really, that I remember. Bradford became less and less involved with the weekly sessions and I started becoming more aware of things they wanted to do that weren't safe. The injections they were giving you, Neo, were blocking your memory, and I was under the impression that was done because you had a high security clearance with the Agency and they wanted to make sure the information you had in your head was protected. They didn't want you dealing with sensitive subjects and not understanding where those thoughts came from. So, the serum was put in place to keep those things 'filed away' in your mind."

"It wasn't until about six months into the whole affair that things started smelling wrong to me. They wanted to increase the dose of a serum that was literally untested. I knew it was totally experimental, but they justified the use of the serum because they said the flashbacks you were having were dangerous to you and to the Agency. They became even more concerned the classified information you possessed in your head would come screaming to the front of your brain before they were ready and short out, or burn out the whole file. They basically wanted to keep you sedated, mentally."

Cayman was listening as the conversation unfolded. "What did you decide to do?"

"I started small, and very carefully, and did a little digging on my own. I found out more about the serum. I knew the serum was Desmond's baby and that he'd lost a dear friend right about the time Neo Weston came into play. As a therapist, I have access to all records of a therapeutic nature and when I read Desmond's file and he spoke of his friend, Justin Markham having died suddenly in a car wreck, I began to feel that the pieces of the puzzle were more displaced than I'd initially thought. The more I dug, the more I uncovered things that were blatantly wrong and actions that were illegal, even for the NSA. I was more than stunned at the death of Justin Markham's family and when I began to put two and two together, I sent the information I'd uncovered in a secure email to Desmond's private email. I didn't really know for absolutely sure Neo Weston and Justin Markham *were* the same person even then, but I was pretty sure they were. In some ways it was a real leap, but a leap that had to be made. I came to realize these people had to be stopped."

Cayman leaned forward, his elbows on the table. "What you've just told us coincides with what we have learned from the Lindgren Papers. It helps to have input from someone who was really there. Thanks for meeting with us."

The three men stood and Leon headed to the door, then stopped abruptly. He turned and looked back at Neo. "I don't know if anyone has told you this, Neo, but I'm sorry. I'm truly sorry for your loss, and for what you've been through on top of that loss. I'm sorry for my part in it. I'm…I'm just so very sorry."

"If you'd known, Leon, you'd have never been party to it. I know that now. And were it not for you and that email to Desmond, who knows where I'd be by now. You saved my life by your actions. I appreciate the apology. I accept it. But you don't need to feel bad. You didn't know."

Leon smiled sadly. "But I should have known." Then he opened the door, walked into the hallway, and shut the door quietly behind him.

Chapter Nine

Desmond gazed at his notebook and frowned. He felt like he'd lost the only opportunity he'd have, for who knows how long, to study how his serum worked as it left a human body. With this last attempted abduction of Neo, it was too dangerous for him to be tested.

There was no way Desmond wanted to see his friend harmed; however disappointing it was. *We know what it does now, and how long it wants to keep its residency in the body, and that's very helpful information.* Desmond sighed as Ciara entered the room.

"What's wrong? More bad news?"

"Someone tried to snatch Neo from the Imaging Department at the hospital."

"No! Is he okay?"

"Yes, fortunately. Cayman interrupted the attempt but the assailant got away. What I can't figure out is *who* knew about the appointment? It had to be our phones, or maybe the house was bugged."

"But the leak could have come from the hospital, too, Desmond."

"Yes, maybe, but that's not as likely."

Desmond reached for his phone and called Neo.

"Hey Neo, it's Desmond. Has our house been swept for bugs?"

"Yes, it was, but it's been a few weeks."

"There is just no way anyone could have known about that appointment I made for you at the hospital unless either our house was bugged or my phone is."

"Let me talk to Cayman and we'll bring a sweeper team and go have a look. If there *is* a bug in there, maybe it will lead us back to who put it there."

The call ended and Desmond continued to think about his serum and how it might be affecting Neo. Hopefully there would be no long-term issues with it; however, the same thought kept returning to his head over and over again. *It wasn't meant to be used that way, and for that long.*

***

Cayman and Neo were at Desmond's home with the sweeper team. They were in the car waiting to hear the results of the sweep, both men lost in thought.

The last attempt at his abduction made Neo wonder if he *should* be in hiding. Was he putting others at risk by being here? If he went to Sophia, would he put her and Mrs. Barbosa both back in danger? He felt like a pariah. It seemed there was nowhere he could be and not be a danger to others. Was this how life was to be for him?

"Cayman, I can't help wondering if I should go into hiding."

Thinking for a minute before he replied, Cayman rested his head in his hand with his elbow on the door. "I'm not sure that would work at this point."

"Yeah, I know what you're going to say. I've been thinking the same thing."

Cayman continued, "Until we find the root of this disease, you'll never be safe, and neither will your friends or your wife. Not finding any hard evidence against them is what's making it so difficult. These guys are professionals. They're agents who know the Bureau and the NSA as well as we do. Just like us, they've been trained to cover their tracks, leave no trace, take out what they brought in. We've found a few bread crumbs, but nothing that would get us a conviction."

Neo was quiet for a few minutes. "Okay, what if we set up a sting? You could use me as bait."

"NO way," replied Cayman, shaking his head. "We have no idea if someone we work with on a daily basis is one of these guys. We set up a sting and rogue agents give away the plan and you disappear again. We can't risk that, Neo."

Neo sighed and turned to look out his window. Still staring out the window he began again, slowly. "True, but what if you and I were the only ones who knew about it? What if we set it up, got everything ready and then let it slip that I was going to, say, go to the park. What if we set it up like you and I had a parting of the ways. I stomp off in anger and go to a predetermined place, and we'll see who comes after me. It could work."

"Yeah, and a million things could go wrong." Cayman's eyes grew distant, like he saw something miles ahead but couldn't quite make it out. "But, still, if we *could* pull this off, we could maybe get a lead that would give us names."

"We've got the Lindgren Papers, but they're names of double agents. And though that is incredibly useful, they are not necessarily the same agents who were involved with my situation. We need something that will help with *this* investigation, agreed?"

"Absolutely. I feel like this investigation has stalled. We need teams to be out there chasing down leads, and we don't have any leads. I don't think I've ever had a more frustrating assignment."

The car fell silent again and eventually three of the sweeper team exited Desmond's home. As they came down the walk, Neo lowered his window.

"What's the news?" he said to the lead agent.

"They had bugs in every room." He held up a small plastic bag and Neo took it, handing it to Cayman.

"We may be able to get something off of those, you think?"

"I sure hope so," replied Cayman. Then turning to the agent outside the car, he said, "Thanks, guys. Lock it up when you leave, okay?"

"Will do, sir."

The men returned to the house and Cayman and Neo drove back into D.C. to get the bugs examined in the FBI lab.

"How do you know if you can trust anyone in the labs?" It was a good question and Cayman wasn't sure how to answer it.

"I guess we stay there and watch them work." Which was exactly what they did.

Cayman told the techs he'd always wanted to see how they made their ingenious discoveries and they were happy to show him. There were no fingerprints on any of the small units, and he'd expected that. What he'd hoped to find, however, was some form of manufacturing imprint that would allow them to trace the purchase, but there was nothing. Every piece of evidence led them nowhere and Cayman was becoming more and more frustrated.

After the lab work was done, the two men left the lab and returned to Cayman's office. Neo was quiet, apparently deep in thought.

"Where'd you go? Are you still in there or am I sitting with an empty shell?"

Neo looked up and shook his head. "I don't know, I just can't get over thinking I'm a hindrance to this investigation. How can you protect me and get the job done at the same time. I need to either branch out on my own or go into hiding myself."

"Yeah, right. We've seen how well that branching out on your own works for you, Mr. Pinters. They've got voice recognition units and they'll find you one way or another. As tall as you are, you could disguise yourself any way you want, but your height gives you away every time. You know that."

"I know, but there has to be an answer. We have to get some leads from somewhere." Neo's frustration was showing right along with Cayman's.

"I've been thinking about that," mused Cayman. "I think we need to have a chat with Mr. Tipton. We still need to address that trip wire issue."

Neo agreed and within the hour Tipton was, once again, sitting in an interrogation room with Neo and Cayman watching him from observation.

"He's still so cocky," said Neo. "What happened to him? He was always so...*not* cocky. I wouldn't say he was humble, but his confidence level seemed real. Looking back, I have to wonder."

"Same old story. Bad guy plays the part of a good guy, gets caught, the real guy is seen clearly for the first time. We see it all the time."

"Yeah, I suppose, but it just never stops being such a letdown," said Neo, shaking his head. "This guy was a leader with people who looked up to him. I guess the only way to save face is with an "I never cared anyway" attitude."

"I'd be willing to bet his rogue team is going to try something. We'd better be prepared." Cayman stared through the glass at the prisoner, his eyes distant and thoughtful.

They left observation and went the short distance to the interrogation room where Tipton waited. They opened the door and Neo wanted to puke at the grand smile that awaited them.

"It's just too weird to be on this side of the table, you know?" said Tipton, acting like nothing had happened to cause this turn of events.

Neo and Cayman said nothing, and sat down across from him at the small table. Cayman quietly leafed through the file he'd carried in with him.

"You wanna explain the trip wires?" Cayman slid the photo of the wires across the table.

Tipton smiled the same wide, friendly smile that greeted them earlier. "I figured you'd see that. Any agent worth their salt would have."

Cayman didn't smile. "And if we hadn't been 'worth our salt?'"

Tipton chuckled and raised his hands, imitating a large explosion. "Boom."

"I see, so what would that have accomplished?"

"All the evidence would be gone. No link to me, to Elsa, no evidence." His eyes focused on Neo. "I'm surprised you're still here."

"Why's that?" Neo never flinched, just stared at Tipton.

"You should be back undercover by now."

Neo stayed put, but it took all the self-control he possessed. It was infuriating how little the rogue agents cared about what they'd done to him, but he couldn't allow himself to get sucked in. He *wouldn't* allow it.

"Who ordered the grab?" Cayman's eyes never left Tipton's.

"At the hospital? Hmm...I'm afraid I really don't know."

"I see," replied Cayman. "Poor guy. They've shut you out. You're a liability to them now, so you're out of the loop. That must be hard to live with."

"If I'm out of the loop, why did I know about the grab, then?"

"Yeah, why did you know?" Cayman smirked. This was where his boyish face came in especially handy in an interrogation. He looked like a smart-mouthed teen, and to an adult, there was nothing more irritating.

Tipton realized he'd been sucked in, but his pride got the best of him.

"I'm *not* shut out. They make no decisions without me." He gritted his teeth and the muscles in his jaw worked back and forth.

Neo laughed a little harder than he should have, but he couldn't help it. "Yeah, when I'm in control of a situation, I always get mad like that. It helps me think clearly."

"You just keep looking over your shoulder, Weston. You're gonna wish you had eyes in the back of your head."

Neo leaned forward, his elbows on the table as his eyes bore into Tipton's. "Haven't you heard? They're already there."

Chapter Ten

The time is two a.m. and Tipton is asleep in his cell. A gloved hand cuts the power to the monitor for all the CCTV cameras in the FBI detainment area. At the same time the monitor goes dark, a small device rolls down the hall and into the guard station. The sole night guard jumps to grab it, but the sleep agent is already seeping into the air and the guard falls unconscious. There is no movement from Tipton. A man in a gas mask makes his way through the thick smoke and moves quickly to the prisoner's cell.

Raising a suppressed gun, he fires two shots into the sleeping body on the bed and quickly runs back down the hall. Within seconds alarms sound, and agents race to the cellblock.

***

Sophia sat curled up on the couch trying to read, but not having much luck. Her mind wandered constantly to Neo, and how she felt broken in half in his absence. It was a strange feeling for her, as she'd never thought she'd ever 'need' anyone, and it wasn't really even a need. It was a want. They were husband and wife for a reason, and that reason was so they could be together forever, never separated again.

It was a bit of a shock to discover not only what Neo did for a living, but the level of intelligence and expertise he had in his job. She'd always known how smart he was, though he worked very hard at downplaying it. His reasoning powers were amazing, and his ability to stay calm when she was ready to pick up an easy chair with her bare hands and toss it through a window was even more impressive. He could calm her down with a touch, and that same touch could light a fire in her that lasted for days. All she had to do was close her eyes and she could feel the warmth of his arms around her, the soft, gentle calm of his voice. Oh, how she loved this man.

I guess that's what it's like to really love someone.

Even with the pain of separation she felt, she'd marry him all over again if she had to. She worried less about his safety after having seen him in action, but still, no one was invincible. She still hoped he would be extra careful.

She remembered watching him come for her, seeing him so confident, so self-assured and that made her miss him all the more. How could someone with the ability to kill like that still be the gentle, compassionate soul she knew him to be? Sophia sighed, a deep, troubled sigh. He said he'd return to her, and she knew he would.

"Okay, Mrs. Neo," came the familiar voice of Mrs. Barbosa, "you come and eat lunch. You disappear completely if you don't eat. Not good for you. You will have babies one day, and need to be strong. You come and eat."

Sophia chuckled and lay her book down on the end table. She stood and stretched. "I'm coming Mrs. Barbosa, I'm coming."

"And boys come, too. They too skinny. Need food."

The thought made a laugh escape her mouth as she considered Patrick and Sam Richards. They were anything but skinny. Buff, yes. Hot, definitely, but not skinny. Maybe since Mrs. Barbosa was comparing them to Neo, they appeared skinny to her. Sophia giggled. In Sophia's heart there was no comparison. "I'll get them," she said, walking to the door.

"Hey guys, Mrs. Barbosa is insisting you come and eat. She says you're too skinny."

Patrick's deep blue eyes considered his younger brother. "This fatty? Are you kidding me? We both barely fit through this door."

Sam laughed and elbowed his brother. Most unlike the other two, Sam's dark eyes and hair made him look adopted. Cayman and Patrick looked every bit like the typical California water doggies, but Sam's dad always teased that he was going to check into the lineage of the milkman to make sure Sam was *truly* a Richards. When Sam was younger he always wondered what that meant. Shaking his head at the memory, Sam trailed his brother into the kitchen.

A 'Mrs. Barbosa lunch' was as big as her dinners. She was an amazing cook and Sophia, Patrick and Sam ate all that was put in front of them. Though Sophia ate much less, she still ate it all. Sophia enjoyed the banter between the two brothers, even encouraged it. Their joking and teasing each other was a wonderful break in her otherwise boring day.

"Did I ever tell you about how Sam got a major butt kicking from our boss one time?"

She'd heard the story several times, but each time Patrick told it, the facts were just a little different. Different enough to make it interesting no matter how often he told the story.

"Oh, come on Patrick, she's heard that a hundred times," moaned Sam, rolling his eyes. "As a matter of fact, here…let me tell it. You see, Sophia, I was an independent little jerk who liked to work alone. Until one dark rainy night when I got my butt kicked by some thugs and almost died…but didn't…and I think my boss was kind of disappointed to see that I lived so *he* kicked my butt. There was an awful lot of butt kicking going on those days and it always seemed to be my butt, because, like I said, I was an independent little jerk. But just look at me now! What's not to love, eh Patrick?"

Sophia started laughing as Patrick broke into the story.

"You *know* it didn't go down like that," he protested.

"You go work," called Mrs. Barbosa with a smile. "I hear story so many times it in my dreams. Out with you…you no tell truth, not either of you. Out!"

The brothers hurried to the front door, arguing all the way about the fine points of the story.

Mrs. Barbosa watched them go with a kindly smile on her face. "They good boys. Like Mr. Neo. They good boys."

They were good men, and Sophia was thankful they were the ones to guard her and Mrs. Barbosa. They were easy to talk to, fun to have around and they did their jobs like the experts they were. Sophia had no complaints, except that she was without her love. Neo would complete the picture, but in reality, if Neo was here, she wouldn't need Patrick and Sam. They could then go home to their wives, who she was sure were missing their husbands as much as she was missing Neo. Sophia was getting a clearer and clearer picture as to the sacrifices the families of men in these lines of work make. She hoped she never had to do this again, but she knew there would be short assignments in the future where Neo would be gone. She could handle the short hops, she just hoped he would never have to be gone for months.

      Lunch hadn't really agreed with her and she stared out the window wondering if she was going to throw up what she'd eaten. What was the nausea about? Nerves. She was pretty sure she was feeling the effects of having Neo gone so much.

Chapter Eleven

A humble, pale and drawn Wesley Tipton was led into the interrogation room. Learning of the attempt on his life forced him to see how very expendable he was to the rogue team. It also made him see how the organization he'd spent so much time helping put together would rather see him dead than trust he would keep their secrets. He was alone, without backup and support and, by the look of him, it was clear he was feeling that.

Neo and Cayman were, again, watching from observation and could see immediately the impact of the prior evenings attack. The assailant was in custody, an FBI training dropout schooled in the ways of the Bureau. He'd managed to get into the building and then into the cellblock without detection, but Bureau agents had been waiting for him.

For a week prior to the attempted hit, Tipton had been sleeping in a high security cell in a different area. Cayman had several agents he trusted with his own life watch for an attack on Tipton all week, and last night that watch had finally proved fruitful.

Though they'd so far gotten nothing from the attacker, they were hopeful the assassination attempt would make Tipton spill at least a few beans. Once the detention area was secured, Cayman ordered Tipton be awakened and moved into the cell adjoining his previous one. Tipton had hours to stare at the 'dead' blanket-covered dummy. They were about to find out if his brush with death had loosened his tongue.

Cayman and Neo entered the interrogation room and took their places opposite Tipton at the table. Tipton didn't look up or offer any smug smiles; he just stared at his hands in silence.

Cayman started right in. He laid out several eight-by-ten glossies of Tipton's original cell after the attack. "Who orders the hits in your organization?"

Tipton continued to stare at his hands.

"You'd be dead now if we hadn't moved you to a safe cell and set the trap that we did. You're not doing yourself any favors by staying silent."

There was still no answer from Tipton. Cayman scooped the pictures up and placed them back in the file. Turning to Neo he said, "Let's go."

They both rose and walked to the door. A voice called softly out from behind them. "Wait."

The two men returned to their places at the table.

"Tristan Bradford is the main player. There are no other Bureau agents involved in the rogue op beside myself. However, some FBI agents are good friends with the NSA agents who *are* involved. Those NSA agents have been instructed to pump their FBI friends for information without being too obvious. They've done well. But you'll get nowhere without Bradford's help. Next, go to my house. There is a wall safe hidden behind a dresser in my bedroom. The dresser is on rollers and easy to move. The safe combination is 13-37-23. In that safe you'll find the names of those involved in the rogue op. Evidence is going to be up to you to find. The documents in my safe should give you some ideas as to where you might find some evidence."

Once Tipton finished speaking, his cuffed hands flew to his mouth and he tossed a pill into his mouth and quickly swallowed. Before either Cayman or Neo could get to him, the pill was gone, and within seconds Tipton was foaming at the mouth. Only a few seconds after that, he was dead.

Events unfolded as if in slow motion. Cayman laid Tipton out on the floor, calling for paramedics while Neo looked on, but it was too late.

Neo couldn't help but think what a sad ending this was. As the paramedics arrived and placed the body in a body bag, all he could do was stare, feeling profoundly sad at the choices Tipton had made over his lifetime, and the effect those choices had on so many.

Cayman came around the table to where Neo was standing. "Do you want to ride over to his house with me? I'm going to have it swept before we go in so we won't leave for an hour or so, will that work?"

"Yeah, yeah, that'll work. I'll just be in the conference room. Come and get me when you're ready to go."

"Will do. I need to write this up, but once I'm done and the sweeper team is done, we'll head out." Cayman studied his friend's face. "Are you all right, Neo? You don't look so good."

"Yeah, yeah. I'm fine. I'm just…I…I don't know how I am. This man stole everything from me, and hurt so many others. I don't even want to think about the deaths he was responsible for. I guess I'm feeling...cheated. But not cheated exactly...I...I really don't know how I feel."

"Just feel everything you need to feel, Neo," said Cayman, clapping Neo on the back. "You'll be so much better off if you do."

Neo nodded and left the room. He went to the conference room and sat down at the large table. He should be excited about the prospect of finding even a drop more evidence against the rogue ops members. They'd gone so long now without any clue as to who was heading the operation, who the major players were and how much information they'd stolen and sold, it seemed like he should be feeling much more joy than he was.

He'd seen so much death in the jobs he'd been asked to do for the Bureau. Always, when he'd taken a life it was to save other lives. But to see someone end their own life, it felt so...violating. How could *he* feel violated at another person's suicide? It made no sense, and maybe violated wasn't the word he wanted, but he couldn't think of another one that made any more sense. Putting the two words, violated and cheated together, he began to understand what he was actually feeling. This man tried to destroy his life, and succeeded in destroying his family. Why should he get a 'get-out-of-life-free' card? He should've been man enough to accept the consequences of his actions, which, when Neo thought about it, would've been death. But it wouldn't have been on Tipton's terms, or on the terms of a hit man. Maybe that's what he couldn't face.

So far away from Sophia, his parents and brother murdered, so much death and destruction. Neo wondered how he was supposed to move forward with his life, how he was supposed to turn and walk away from the dead body they'd taken from the interrogation room, the body that had once housed a living, breathing human being. Now it was a shell, empty and cold. Too much...it was just too much.

Cayman knocked softly on the door and opened it, peeking his head in. "Are you ready to go? The sweeper team is done. They didn't find anything and we've got the go ahead to go in."

Neo rose, surprised at how quickly that hour had gone, and turned to go. Somehow, thinking the whole thing through helped him feel...better. He would move forward, and one day, he and Sophia would have a life together without interruption. He would focus on that life, and get this job done.

Tipton's home was exactly as expected. Fastidiously clean and orderly, just like he was.

With gloved hands, Cayman went directly to the wall safe, as directed by Tipton. He entered the combination and turned the handle. The door opened. There was more money inside, along with a legal-sized manila file folder. Cayman pulled the file slowly from the safe, as if it might break on the way out.

Cayman opened the file, and Neo read the contents over his shoulder. Neo whistled as he read the list of names. "Whoa, there are some high-ups in here, for sure. This is going to take some doing to uncover the evidence needed to convict."

Cayman turned the page and there were several more sheets with dates, references to recorded phone conversations, and payoffs. Cayman turned back to the safe and pulled out the money, placing it in a pile on the floor. The inside of the safe was dark and he pulled a small flashlight off of his belt and pointed the light into the safe. In the far back corner were three flash drives. Cayman pulled them out and looked at Neo.

"This might be the gold we've been looking for. I'll bet they've got those conversations recorded on them, along with the payoffs and dates of contacts, that kind of thing."

Neo shook his head. "Maybe we'll finally get somewhere now. I've known the Lindgren papers were valuable to the Bureau, but they had little to do with this investigation. I always felt Tipton was playing us on that...giving us breadcrumbs but no hard evidence as far as the rogue op went. This is what we've been looking for."

Back in the car and heading to Cayman's office, Cayman was still concerned about Neo. "Are you feeling better? You had me worried there for a bit."

"Yeah, I guess it was all just a little surreal. I mean, I have my life stolen from me, my family is killed, I'm injected with a serum whose sole purpose is to keep me from remembering, my abductors are using *my* family fortune to fund their rogue op, and that's just the *first* year of this whole ordeal. Now, Sophia and I are separated again, I can't even talk to her, and the guy who's responsible for the mess he made of my life just up and kills himself. I guess I'm outraged that he would be such a coward and leave me to find answers to all my hundreds of questions and make my way back to a normal life, a life, by the way, that still eludes me. I just feel angry, and...and...cheated...and used. But, I actually do feel a little better, having said all that. It's just good to dump sometimes."

"That's definitely true. Maybe you'll find some more answers in these drives."

Cayman entered the parking structure and parked. The hairs on the back of Neo's neck suddenly snapped to attention.

"Start the car, Cayman. *NOW*! Get us out of here!"

Chapter Twelve

Cayman started the car, squealed the tires and burned rubber out of the parking garage. Bullets shattered their back window as their car hit the street, narrowly missing other cars. Cayman punched a button on his radio.

"Shots fired! Shots fired! Hoover building parking garage. No injuries. Repeat, no injuries."

Cayman checked his mirror several times, but there seemed to be no one following them. "I think that's weird. Why don't we have a tail? Were they hoping to just kill us and run? I'm assuming they want these drives and this file."

"They must have had someone watching Tipton's house. They were hoping we'd lead them to the information and we did."

Cayman did a few quick turns, doubling back on their route and both men continued checking for a tail. There was nothing. He spoke again into his radio.

"We're heading back to the Hoover Building. Coming in the back way and parking on the street. Get a protection detail out there to wait for us. Have you found any of the shooters in the garage?"

There was static and the agent's voice came back over the radio. "Negative. No shooters found. We'll be waiting for you in the back."

"Can you trust him? Who is he?" Neo's voice was nervous, just like his gut.

Cayman glanced at Neo. "His name is Blake Green and I've always felt I could trust him. We've worked a lot of ops together. I guess we're just going to have to see if he's one of the good guys."

Agent Green was definitely one of the good guys. As he said, he and six other agents were waiting for Cayman and Neo when they arrived. They ushered them into the building and Cayman thanked them, hurrying into his office with Neo close behind.

Sitting down at his desk, Cayman pulled the drives from his pocket and offered them to Neo. "Wanna breathe on them for good luck?"

Neo grinned and shook his head. "Just get them in there. I'm gonna have an ulcer before this is through."

Cayman pushed the first drive into the USB port. He clicked on the file and a list of names popped onto the screen. It was a short list of ten names; all of them top level NSA and/or Government officials. The next page after the names list stated the purpose of their organization. That purpose had only one line on it. Pure and simple, it cleared up the issue as to whether more secrets had been stolen and sold to the highest bidder. The line read: "Secure Justin Weston, acquire formula from his brain when buyer is found, dispose of asset."

Though not the type to display it, Neo's fury would have filled a football stadium. "These men have no conscience. They live to feed their own greed. I'd be willing to bet they were already planning their next op when they had me."

"It's very possible. We owe a lot to Desmond and Leon. If they'd not had the courage to begin this investigation, you'd be dead by now, I'm sure."

Cayman and Neo spent several hours combing over the information from Tipton's safe. It truly was a gold mine, and both men wondered if it wasn't enough to convict every person listed in the file on the drive. However, with something of this magnitude, they wanted to make sure they had solid cases against each person, and that was going to take some digging. In the coming weeks, Cayman and Neo would begin an investigation that would shake the NSA to its core. They'd have lots of help from the already established teams. Neo could finally see a light at the end of the tunnel.

***

Leon Kenning was feeling very good about being back at work, full days now, and about his patient load. It took several weeks for him to come out from under the cloud of his PTSD, but he felt the experience would be invaluable to his clients suffering from the same thing. He would be able to better understand where they were coming from and really help them. He considered the whole affair a blessing more than a curse and poured himself into his work.

Leon was just clearing the paperwork from his desk, having completed the last set of patient notes for the day, when there came a knock at his door. "Come in," he said, without looking up.

The door opened and closed and he glanced up from his paperwork. "How can I..." Rachel Young leaned against the closed door, watching him with green eyes that nearly glowed in the soft light. Her blond hair was a pile on top of her head and as usual, she was dressed with the utmost professional care.

"I just wanted to see how you were doing, Leon. You seem to have gotten your swagger back."

Leon laughed and rose from his chair. "I guess you could say that, though I wasn't aware I *had* a swagger. You're looking stunning this afternoon. What can I do for you?"

Rachel moved toward him, her hips accenting each step. "I just wanted to remind you of the dinner you still owe me. You see, I'm no longer your therapist, and…well… we never did get to finish that dinner…" She smiled a soft, inviting smile and walked up to him, placing her hands on his chest and leaning her hips into him. "…or anything else that I can think of."

"You have a pretty amazing way of inviting yourself to dinner," he said, unable to wipe the amusement off his face. "Just what was it you were in the mood for?"

Her eyes softened and she placed her finger gently on his lips, pulling it slowly down his chin. "Oh, well, they don't serve *that* in a restaurant. And since you're going to need your strength, I suggest we eat first."

Leon's arms went around her waist and he kissed her, the passion boiling inside the two of them. "How do you feel about fast food?"

Chapter Thirteen

Cayman handed Neo the phone. "Keep it short, no names, same as last time."

Neo nodded and grabbed the sat phone. "Hey, how are you?"

Sophia's voice was soft but he was happy to hear her voice in any volume. "I'm good, really good in fact." Neo could hear a smile in her voice. "Are you sitting down?"

"Yes, I am," he said, leaning back in his chair. "What's going on? Are you okay? Are you sick?"

"I guess you could say I'm sick, but it will pass in about three months and then I'll be fine."

"You already know you're going to be sick for three months?" Neo was completely confused. Cayman snickered and turned his back, trying not to let Neo see his face.

"My love, we're going to have a baby."

"A *what?*" Neo bolted upright in his chair. He could feel himself growing pale, but something inside of him exploded. "You're having a baby? A real baby?"

"No, my love, *we're* having a baby, you did help with this you know. And I sure hope it's not going to be a plastic baby, because I hear those are really hard to raise."

"Very funny. I wouldn't care if it was plastic. We're going to have a baby! We're going to be a family! What does our cook think?"

"I haven't told her yet. I wanted you to be the first to know."

"You're amazing. I love you so much. You're just unbelievably amazing. We'll be together soon and we'll watch your belly grow to huge proportions."

"Watch it mister. You'd better tell me everyday how beautiful I look, not how enormous I look."

"That will be easy." Cayman approached, and Neo new it was time to go. "I have to go, but you've just made me happier than I ever thought I could be. You take care of yourself and let our cook help you. She'll be so excited. Don't overdo - I love you!"

Cayman was prying the phone from his hands as the call ended. "Gonna be a daddy, are you?" he asked, grinning at his friend. "There's nothing better in the whole world, other than being a husband."

Neo couldn't believe how he felt, how the pain of the last year had, with one phone call, melted away. He thought of the new life growing inside of the woman he loved like no other. He couldn't wait to hold that new life, to name it, to watch it grow. He couldn't wait to stop calling it 'it.' He felt light, full of life, grateful, excited, he wanted to take Sophia in his arms right this minute and show her exactly how he felt.

Soon. This would all be over soon. They were now on the downhill side of the investigation, and before he knew it, he would be holding his wife in his arms and feeling the new life growing inside her. Life was good. Life was really, really good.

The following day, Neo paid a visit to Emmett, now in the hospital ward at the penitentiary. It was decided Emmett would keep his cover intact should the need arise to use him again. Emmett was taken to a private room with no video equipment. When the door opened Neo was sitting in an easy chair, and rose to greet him.

"I shot you," said Neo, after shaking Emmett's hand and helping him into another easy chair.

"Yes you did, and from what I hear, I need to be very thankful you weren't quite up to speed."

The thought made Neo's stomach lurch. "I could've killed you. Why wasn't I made aware of your standing with the Bureau? That was dangerous."

"We don't need to worry about any of that. It's over and we're both still alive. I've been meaning to tell you something. Something you won't remember doing."

"Oh?"

"After you met with Desmond on the beach that day, you came home and realized with the next injection you received you'd forget about the meeting. So you made a private encrypted file on your computer and hid it away…or so you thought. Should you ever recall doing that, I just wanted you to know that I found the file and deleted it. *They* would've found it, and that would've been the end of Desmond."

"I can't thank you enough for what you did for me. I'm sorry I shot you and sorry I punched you at the zoo. I don't think I was very nice to you at all."

Emmett laughed and waved his hand. It's all in a day's work. You had your job to do and I had mine.

We made it work. I think we were a pretty good team, don't you?"

"I'm going to be a daddy, Emmett. I just found out, and a lot of that is due to you."

"Whoa, wait a minute…I had *nothing* to do with that!"

Neo couldn't help the laughter that bubbled out of him. "Yeah," he said, trying to talk through the laughter. "I guess that came out wrong. What I meant to say is, that wouldn't be happening if you hadn't been so good at your job."

"Seriously, Neo, congratulations. You're going to be a great dad."

"Thanks. Oh, and I have one more question for you. You put that flash drive in the evidence lockup at the FBI didn't you?"

"Yes, guilty as charged. I was instructed by Tipton to go to his safe and put a file in there. He totally trusted me, and that was good for the investigation. I did put the file in there, but not until I did a good search of what was in the safe. The file was sealed, and there was no way I could open it without destroying the seal on it. I took one of the drives, hoping he wouldn't notice it was gone. He didn't. I don't think he had a chance to see it was missing. I believe he was certain he'd been discovered and was trying to figure out a way to cover his tracks."

"Well, it was genius of you to do that, and incredibly dangerous. You could've been discovered."

"It was no big deal. I knew the risks, and they were totally worth it. You know, it was a real pleasure working with you, Neo. Let's do it again sometime."

"Yeah, only next time, let's have you be the guy that has his face redone, eh?"

"Okay, but I want the money and the lifestyle, too."

"You got it."

Epilogue

The list of ten names stared up at Neo from the page he'd printed off the computer. Ten names. Ten people who'd ruined his life, just to get their hands on a code in his head. He still wished he'd never thought of that code, never realized its implications.

Now the work began in earnest. It was time to start the hunt, and one by one bring down those responsible for the havoc they'd caused in his life. Desmond was on the mend, able to walk now without a walker, with the use of crutches. Ciara was back to work, things were returning to some sense of normalcy, except for Neo and Sophia.

Emmett was also working once again and feeling good as new. The guilt Neo felt over nearly killing him was gone. It hadn't been his fault, he knew it and Emmett knew it.

Still concerned for her safety, the Bureau kept Sophia secreted away with Mrs. Barbosa. Even Neo didn't know where they were, and he liked it that way. Neo and Sophia were going to be parents, and it was more important than ever now to keep her safe. She carried their future inside her.

Neo stared down at the names. One by one they would be extracted from the NSA and made to pay for their crimes. Together Neo and Cayman would continue their work of weeding them out. They would collect evidence and keep a low profile so the rogue ops members wouldn't know they were being hunted. Though some had already run, they would be found. It was a promise Neo made to himself, and to his unborn child. He would make the world safe for his little family, at least safe from the greed of these individuals. There would always be bad guys, but once this cancer was excised, the bad guys wouldn't be after Neo. The sooner he got this encryption code out to the public, the sooner he'd be free to have his family back.

Let the games begin. Neo was ready to end this.

To be continued...

Chapter One
Extracted, Book Two
Duty and Deception Series

Tristan Bradford lay in bed; the beauty beside him very still, eyes closed. He rolled onto his side and admired her, outlining the shape of her perfect lips with his finger and then tracing the outline of her jaw. He sighed and rolled onto his back. Strange, how good it felt to have someone to tell his escape plan to. It clarified the weak places in his thinking and helped him find ways around the holes in his view of things. She'd been invaluable. How it grated on him to see his mistakes out in the open, though, and from what he'd heard from his own mouth as he laid his plan out before the beauty beside him, his errors were blaring.

A lifetime of work, down the tube. He'd screwed up, he knew it, and he was certain the Bureau knew it. He'd heard nothing of any investigation as yet, however. With a little luck, maybe there wouldn't be one. *That idiot Tipton had best kept his mouth shut.* The lid on Tipton's death was tighter than a sealed coffin. *Why?*

The Feds knew something. They had to. It irritated him, after all these years of being in control of the flow of information, to now be shut out. As Deputy Director of Research for the National Security Agency, Tristan was made aware of every interesting piece of new technology out there, when it came to national security. Not only access to the technology, he also had sources in every corner and the ability to pay them for information he needed. Now, he knew nothing. His pipeline of information had gone dry, and how much the Feds knew of his 'activities' or how much they didn't know was a mystery to him. He didn't like mysteries.

The Justin Markham fiasco had been handled poorly. Yes, it was a complicated op, and it seemed at every turn it became *more* complicated. However, the sale of Markham's 'fire sale' prevention algorithm would have capped off the fortune Tristan already possessed, ensuring a more than comfortable existence for his remaining days.

He shouldn't have trusted Tipton, should've known he'd make a mess of the whole affair. Now Justin Markham was running around out there with a new face, a new name and a new life, supposedly, and Tristan had nothing. He had less than nothing. How in the world had his life gotten this messed up, anyway?

Tristan examined the marks on the neck of the woman beside him as he picked up his phone from the nightstand and dialed the number of his cleaner. His evening's companion had been lovely, everything he'd wanted her to be. Killing her had been regrettably necessary, for the simple reason if they're dead they don't tell. Anything.

The phone on the other end was ringing.
"Yeah."

"Room 548. The Grand. Body disposal, evidence removal. Sanitize. Money will be under her pillow. I'll be out of the room in forty-five minutes. Room key will be in the usual place."

"Done."

The call ended. He rose from the bed and went into the bathroom, grabbing clean clothes on the way. As he stepped into the shower, his mind wandered back to his early days with the NSA. He'd been straight as an arrow, until the day one William Grantham approached him with a proposal. He'd always respected Bill Grantham, actually wanted to pattern his career after him, and in the beginning he'd been flattered by the trust Grantham placed in him for these 'special' assignments. By the time Tristan figured out what the man was *really* up to, not only was Tristan also deeply involved in illegal activities. He was hooked on the highs that came with it, the money, the lies, the promised lifestyle.

Grantham, now in prison for murder and treason, had been with the Bureau at the time and needed a contact at the NSA he felt he could rely on. He invited Tristan to be a 'delivery boy' for everything from envelopes to packages. Opening anything given him would mean his death; and Grantham had made that part very clear. For each delivery, he was paid five hundred dollars.

As time went on, Grantham's requests became more specific, more…illegal…and his payments had increased substantially. Tristan remembered exactly when he'd realized there was no backing out. Not that he'd wanted to, but in retrospect, he definitely should have. Instead, he watched and he learned how the 'business' was run. He paid special attention to where

Grantham's lists of sources was kept, who was in the know and who wasn't.

When Grantham was arrested, Tristan felt it was not just his right , but his responsibility to pick up the man's illegal affairs and take the profits from them himself. At first he was concerned Grantham's trail would lead to Tristan but after a few months of sweating and wondering, everything calmed back down and it was business as usual.

Tristan had millions tucked away in off-shore accounts. He could have retired years ago, but he'd become addicted to the thrill of espionage, the electrifying effect of watching secrets and money change hands, the covert meetings and whispered plans.

Tristan couldn't even use his money in the States. If he lived beyond the income afforded him by his position at the NSA, he'd arouse suspicion and it would all be over. So he'd waited, patiently, deciding at one point he'd retire and move out of the country. Then Justin Markham showed up, and Tristan saw the opportunity for the score of a lifetime. Markham's magic algorithm was to be his last deal, his last big sale. He'd had no idea how true that would be.

The sale never happened; Markham couldn't even remember how to tie his own shoes after Tipton was done with him. Tristan was certain the priceless encryption code, now locked in the head of Neo Weston, would never see the light of day. It was gone, thanks to the misuse of the serum they'd injected him with.

Tristan's initial involvement happened because Markham talked about *giving* the code away! Making it available to every business and household in the world. What was he thinking? There were obscene amounts of money to be made with that code.

Markham had no business head whatsoever. Now no one would have that goldmine. It still irritated him to think of it.

He turned off the shower, dried and dressed and returned to the bed. He sat down beside the body of his paid escort. Now the question was how to get rid of the body. He shouldn't have used his credit card to order her 'services.' Bad call. There'd been a lot of those lately. He didn't know if they were tracking him yet, or if he'd even been included in their list of suspects. It all depended on what Tipton told them, and no one was privy to that information.

It shouldn't matter if the FBI found her in his room or not. But why should he hand them evidence on a platter? Tristan was glad he'd called the cleaner and looked forward to his upcoming flight.

He was heading out of the country, happy to be rid of the responsibilities of keeping so much hidden. Now, his life would be ever so much easier. He could come and go as he pleased and live a life of privilege. He'd been thinking about where he wanted to live. With the amount of money he now possessed, he could live anywhere. He could have homes in several different countries. Spain was nice, or so he'd heard. And he liked Italy, although, the German countryside was supposed to be lovely as well. Just so many options it made him smile.

Tristan stood and grabbed his coat, briefcase and roll bag. He could wait at the airport, hidden in the first class lounge, until boarding. Though he'd not planned for it all to end this way, he was happy to be free of the NSA. With one last glance around the room to be sure he'd not left anything, he opened the door and left, placing the 'Do Not Disturb' sign on the knob and closing the door behind him. He slipped the key just under the door where it couldn't be seen, but could easily be slid out if it's position was known.

Tristan stepped off the elevator and saw a group of six FBI agents at the front desk. He took a smooth but quick left turn into the lounge and pulled out his cell phone.

"Yeah."

"Are you in the room?"

"Yes."

"Get out now. Forget about sanitizing, just get the girl out now. Take the service elevator and go out the back way. There are agents in the lobby on their way up to you within the next few minutes. Go. Now."

He'd recognized Cayman Richards and Neo Weston immediately upon exiting the elevator. He'd seen the other four around, as well, but never spoken to them nor had any interaction with them. Tristan peered around the corner into the lobby and watched as Cayman, obviously the leader, spoke to the clerk and nodded, showing his badge before the clerk gave him a room key. He was certain the key was to his room. How could they have found his trail so quickly?

He ducked back to avoid detection. The men entered the elevator and disappeared behind the closing doors. Tristan hurried out the front door and hailed a taxi. Winter was setting in and the rain and snow mix poured from the sky.

"Dulles, please. Make it fast and I'll pay you double." He wiped the water from his shoulders and from the front of his coat, then shook the water from his hat onto the seat beside him.

"Yes, sir!" The taxi sped away from the curb and blended into traffic. Tristan watched the hotel disappear in the side mirror. *That was a close one.*

Tristan wondered if the FBI would be watching the airports. He hadn't thought of that until now. *That's not very professional of me, I should be thinking ahead better than this.* He never had to worry about who was watching what, he'd had people to do that. Now he was on his own. Still, he'd not done too badly, he had his passport ready, fake name, fake ID, if he kept his head down, it was quite possible he'd make it out of this without any problems. Knowing Cayman Richards--that was a really big 'if.'

Picking up his cell phone once more, he auto-dialed one more number.

"It's me, I'm on my way to the airport. You have my flight information, check for the gate. Be ready. You won't have a lot of time."

Tristan hung up the phone and allowed himself to relax...a little. Everything was in place. *If the cleaner didn't make it out of the room in time that's his problem. And who cares if Cayman's little team finds the body. I'm out of here anyway.*

Checking his luggage at the curb, Tristan hurried into the airport, his eyes watching every corner. He couldn't keep looking over his shoulder, as that would make him look suspicious, so he hurried through the security check and went directly to the first class lounge. He'd traveled enough from this airport, he knew exactly where it was.

Once inside the lounge, he found a quiet corner and pulled a newspaper from the seat beside him, burying himself behind it, peeking out every so often to check new arrivals. The lounge was relatively full, which helped his cause quite well. It was easier to hide when you weren't the only person in the room.

From the corner of his eye, Tristan saw the clerk at the desk peer around the corner at him and, once eye contact was made, immediately disappeared. That was his cue to leave.

He slowly folded the newspaper and lay it beside him on the seat. He rose casually and sauntered slowly through the lounge and out the door. Looking back, he saw the lounge attendant pick up the phone. He'd been recognized.

Eventually, Tristan headed to his gate, hiding under his hat and keeping his overcoat on. He arrived at the gate just as the plane was boarding and entered without any issues. Once he set his foot on the passenger boarding bridge, he looked to the end of the bridge and saw his man in charge of 'plan B' waiting right where he said he'd be. Plan B was a go.

Other books by JL Redington

Juvenile Series (8-13):

The Esme Chronicles:

A Cry Out of Time
Pirates of Shadowed Time
A View Through Time
A River In Time

Broken Heart Series:

The Lies That Save Us
Solitary Tears
Veiled Secrets
Softly She Leaves
Loves New Dawning

Passions in the Park:

Love Me Anyway
Cherish Me Always
Embrace Me Forever

Duty and Deception:
Novella Series

Erased
Entangled
Enlightened

Extracted
Eradicated

Come join me on
Facebook: Author JL Redington
Email: contact@jlredington.com
Twitter: @jlredington

Made in the USA
Charleston, SC
02 July 2015